'Are you alwa

Sam's blue eyes retu

'Only when provoked.' Furiously Jaimie tried to free her arm, but his grasp merely tightened, drawing her closer.

'I do seem to bring out the worst in you, don't I?' he said evenly. 'I'm not saying I'm not grateful.'

'I don't want your gratitude, Doctor,' she said heatedly. 'All I'm asking is that you let me do my share. Judge me on results, not on your own obvious prejudices. Forget I'm a woman.'

Jean Evans was born in Leicester and married shortly before her seventeenth birthday. She has two married daughters and several grandchildren. She gains valuable information and background for her Medical Romances™ from her husband, who is a senior nursing administrator. She now lives in Hampshire, close to the New Forest, and within easy reach of the historic city of Winchester.

Recent titles by the same author:

HEART IN HIDING

RULES OF ENGAGEMENT

BY
JEAN EVANS

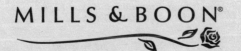

MILLS & BOON®

First published in Great Britain 2000
Harlequin Mills & Boon Limited,
Eton House, 18-24 Paradise Road, Richmond, Surrey TW9 1SR

© Jean Evans 2000

ISBN 0 263 82240 0

Set in Times Roman 10½ on 12 pt.
03-0006-49016

Printed and bound in Spain
by Litografia Rosés, S.A., Barcelona

CHAPTER ONE

JAIMIE GRANT edged her car out of the mainstream of traffic into a lay-by and switched off the engine. She felt tired and the wintry afternoon light had gradually begun to fade, making concentration more difficult.

Hunting in the glove compartment, she drew out a map, unfolded it and, having poured a cup of coffee from the Thermos on the seat beside her, began to study the criss-cross of lines which would eventually bring her to Felldale.

Her fingers traced the route and a glance at her watch showed two o'clock. She had made good time despite the sudden downpour and a stop for a cup of tea just north of Newbury. With a bit of luck she should make her destination easily by teatime.

Draining the coffee, she flicked the dregs out of the window and shivered. The afternoon air already struck with a deepening chill, heralding a frost.

Stifling a yawn, Jaimie switched on the car radio. 'Followed by more snow in the north,' announced a voice.

'Oh, great. I'd rather not know that, thank you very much.' Silencing the radio again, she screwed the top back on the Thermos and freshened up quickly with a tissue, using the vanity mirror to flick a comb through her hair.

The reflection that stared back at her showed an oval face framed by chestnut hair, which she had tied up into a ponytail, making her look ridiculously younger than her twenty-six years.

It had been the cause of a certain amount of teasing at medical school. Not that she had minded. It had all been good-natured teasing, but a frown momentarily etched its way into her forehead. She could see that it might become a problem, but right now she was too excited to worry about it.

Jaimie smiled slightly as her glance fell upon the letter in her open bag. She had read it a dozen times but a tiny tremor of excitement still ran through her as she studied it again. 'Dear Dr Grant...' Even now she still found it difficult to get used to the idea that she had actually passed her final exams, had achieved the goal she had dreamed of for so long.

Folding the letter back into her bag, she restarted the engine and eased her way back into the traffic. Looking back on it now, those years of dedicated training at a large teaching hospital still had something of a dreamlike quality about them.

It began to rain heavily again and she set the windscreen wipers in motion, hoping it wasn't going to snow before she reached Felldale. It had been a long winter and a promise of spring had proved to be tantalisingly brief. Still, it couldn't last for ever. Another week and it would be April.

The reminder had come from her father when he had first broached the subject of the job to her and she had jokingly responded that the north of England in the depths of winter wasn't the ideal place to be.

Martin Grant had viewed his daughter with a twinkle in his eye as he'd made a stabbing motion in her direction with his pipe.

'You're just scared, my girl, looking for an excuse

to avoid taking up your responsibilities. Well, you can't run away for ever. You worked hard for that qualification, Jaimie. What was it all for? It's time you started putting it to good use. Good doctors are hard to come by.'

Her blue eyes were suddenly serious as she faced him. 'Oh, Dad, I know you're right. I've been using any excuse not to have to make a decision. It's just that…well, I know it's stupid but now that the crunch has finally come I'm nervous. I don't expect you to understand.' She grinned. 'It's a big world out there. I'm just beginning to realise how sheltered we were in medical school and now, suddenly, it's all for real.'

Contrary to her expectations, her father didn't laugh. He settled back in his chair, looked around the well-used surgery and frowned. 'As a matter of fact, I understand perfectly. I wasn't always a GP, you know. I had to start somewhere thirty years ago. I was pretty damn scared, too, when I first came here.'

'You were?' Jaimie stared at him, unaware of how alike they were, not only in temperament but in looks, too, at that moment, even though her father's hair was now liberally sprinkled with grey. 'I find it hard to imagine.'

'Why?' He smiled. 'Medicine isn't the easiest of professions. The work is damned hard. The rewards are pretty varied and the responsibilities increase as patients get to know you and put their trust in you.'

Jaimie gave a slight laugh. 'I'm not sure that this is making me feel any better.'

'I'm not saying you won't make mistakes. They happen. Pray God, rarely. But doctors are fallible, Jaimie, human beings. We don't have all the answers. We do the best we can. Sooner or later you'll find all this out for yourself but you've got to take that first step.' He shrugged. 'Otherwise what were all those years of training for?'

Jaimie went to stand behind his chair and put her arms round his shoulders. 'It's what I've always wanted to do, you know that?'

'I should. I'm the one who taught you to bandage your dolls.'

She laughed. 'I practised on the dog, too, don't forget—and the cat.'

Martin Grant took the pipe from his mouth. 'Well, it's not dolls any more, is it? It's for real now and you've got to start somewhere. Are you sure don't want to specialise?'

'No.' She shook her head, quite definite about that. 'I like the idea of working and living in a community, getting to know the people. I've always felt the hospital system was a bit like a conveyor belt.'

'I know what you mean. I've always felt the same way.'

'But you've never regretted becoming a GP?'

'Never.' He frowned and patted her hand. 'I'm only sorry there isn't scope for another partner here. You know there's nothing I'd like more than to have you with me.'

'I know.' Jaimie pressed a hand over his. 'But it's probably best that I start somewhere else. You're right, I need to learn to stand on my own feet.'

'You haven't found anything so far?'

'No.' She frowned, pushing a strand of hair behind her ear in a gesture he recognised well. 'I've made some enquiries, of course, but nothing has come up so far. There's a locum's job up in Scotland for about six weeks.'

'Hmm.' He foraged through the desk for a letter, which he handed to her. 'This may interest you. Read it. See what you think. In a way it might be the hand of providence.'

He sat in silence as she moved to sit in the chair and scanned the single page. Her glance flew up to meet his.

'Oh, Dad, I can't believe it. Not Uncle Jon. Why didn't you tell me?'

'You had other things to worry about.' He frowned. 'Apparently the heart attack happened about a month ago. His partner wrote to tell me.'

'Is…is it very bad?'

'According to young Paige, it would have been enough to finish anyone less determined.'

Her face paled and she studied the letter again. 'Paige?'

'Sam Paige. Jon's partner.'

'So he's written to you again?'

'A couple of times. He's been keeping me up to date on his progress, but I can judge for myself that Jon must be feeling better if he managed to write that.'

The handwriting was less firm than she remembered but still recognisable, and Jaimie found herself wondering why doctors in particular, and herself no less, were always notorious for their barely legible scrawls.

'He says he isn't going to be back at work for at least another three months and then only on light duties.'

'Which presumably means no night or emergency calls.' Martin frowned. 'That's why he wrote.' He gestured towards the page. 'He says it's a busy practice and it seems that Sam has taken over the entire case load until now. Obviously Jon feels it's more than one man can reasonably be expected to handle for any length of time. Which is why he decided it's time to get a locum in.'

There was a brief silence during which Jaimie sensed what was coming, and was proved right when he said simply, 'You could do it, Jaimie. How about it? It would put Jon's mind at rest.'

She laughed awkwardly. 'But I don't have the experience, Dad, and I don't know anything about this…Sam Paige.'

'Does that matter? You know Jon. It would help to stop him worrying. Isn't that what counts?'

'Yes, of course it is, and I'd like to help, you know that.' She smiled. 'I haven't seen Uncle Jon for…it must be five years. I used to love it when we went to Felldale on holiday when I was small.' Her smile faded. 'In a way I almost feel I owe it to Uncle Jon. After all, he first put the idea of going into medicine into my head, but…' She frowned. 'Dad I'd hate to let him down and more to the point is the fact that this Sam Paige doesn't know me. He might not like the idea of having a newly qualified doctor as his locum.'

'Well, there's one way to find out. Why not write and ask him?' Her father applied a match to his pipe and puffed in silence for a moment, looking at her in silence through a haze of smoke.

There was a hint of a challenge in his eyes. 'This could be the somewhere you have to start, my dear, and it will help Jon and you'd be doing me a big favour as well.'

And how could she argue with logic like that? She

opened her mouth and closed it again, but that night she wrote the letter, outlining her qualifications and experience to date. She posted it next morning before she could change her mind, then promptly forgot about it so that when, a few days later, a reply fluttered through the letter box she had to fight a sudden feeling of unreasoning panic.

The reply was brief almost to the point of being curt.

Dear Dr Grant,
Dr Reynolds assures me that he has every confidence in your ability to assist in covering this practice during his absence. I shall, therefore, expect to see you in a week's time. You will, of course, be aware that whilst Felldale is a rural community patient numbers increase as the tourist season advances, so that you will be expected to work whatever hours are deemed necessary.

The signature was a large, indecipherable scrawl.

Sam Paige sounded arrogant, Jaimie decided as she read the letter again. He certainly didn't sound as if he would be easy to work with. On the other hand, it would only be for three months.

Sighing, she rose to her feet. Surely she could cope with that? After all, it seemed a small price to pay for everything Jon Reynolds and her father had done for her over the years.

But that didn't prevent the nagging doubts resurfacing now as her car ate up the miles, bringing her inexorably closer to Felldale.

The car sped easily enough along the motorway before she turned off. The towns gradually gave way to greener, more hilly countryside. The weather changed, too. What had been a light drizzle gave way to a flurry of snow as she headed north and finally spotted the turning for Felldale.

The streets of the small market town were crowded with shoppers and Jaimie found herself gazing at a fascinating blend of both ancient and modern, tea-shops and antique markets vying with large stores, all catering for a huge tourist trade. Smiling, she promised herself a return visit when she had time to wander through the many alleyways.

It was several seconds before she registered the distant sound of tyres screeching. It was only as she slowed to glance towards the gathering crowd that she realised there had been an accident and someone was obviously hurt.

The traffic had slowed and Jaimie felt a momentary rush of anger as she saw drivers winding down their windows, morbid curiosity on their faces.

And I'll bet no one has thought to call an ambulance, she thought grimly, as she brought her own car to a halt. Her initial instinct not to get involved was banished as she saw the vehicle's crumpled metalwork and a blood-spattered figure slumped over the steering-wheel.

She watched, horrified, as someone ran towards it, hauled open the door and began to try to lift the injured man out. Instinctively she swung her car door open and got out, running towards the spot. Broken glass littered the road. She sidestepped it carefully.

'Don't do that,' she called out sharply. 'Can't you see he's hurt? You might make things worse.'

The man turned to look at her. 'We can't just leave him.'

'He may have internal injuries. You could do more harm if you try to move him before we know what the extent of the damage is.'

There was a murmured ripple of approval from the growing crowd. The man muttered something and moved aside as Jaimie reached into the car, feeling swiftly for the injured man's pulse. She breathed a sigh of relief. At least he was still alive, though he was pale, his breathing was worryingly shallow and he was losing blood from a head wound. At the very least she guessed that he probably had concussion.

'I'm a doctor,' she explained quickly, sensing a tiny flicker of resentment. 'He's alive but we need to get him to hospital. Has anyone called an ambulance?' She moved round the car and eased herself carefully into the passenger seat, making it easier to carry out a gentle examination.

'I'll see to it, Doctor.' Someone sprinted away. She didn't look up to see who it was. Her attention was focused on the man who was slowly, painfully, beginning to regain consciousness.

Jaimie shivered, suddenly aware that the temperature had dropped and that it was beginning to snow heavily. She was glad she had decided to wear sensible jeans and a chunky high-necked sweater for travelling. Gently she ran her fingers over the injured man's arm. His eyes flickered open and he groaned as he tried to sit up.

'Try not to move,' she urged softly.

'Where…?' He stared at her with understandable confusion. 'What happened?'

'There was an accident.'

He brushed a hand against his head, making contract with a trickle of blood. 'I don't… Oh, yes, there was someone…a child.' He glanced up at Jaimie. 'My God, he's not…?'

Jaimie shook her head as she hunted in her pocket for a clean handkerchief, folded it into a pad and used it to try to stem the worryingly persistent flow of blood.

'It's all right. If it's any consolation, you're the only casualty.'

He gave an audible sigh. 'I didn't see him until it was too late. He just shot out from between those parked cars. I don't know how I missed him.'

'It wouldn't have been your fault if you hadn't.' Someone in the crowd pressed forward. 'Wearing roller-boots he was. Straight across the road. Didn't so much as look.'

The injured man frowned. 'I tried to stop.' He moistened his lips with his tongue. 'As long as he's all right.'

'He's long gone,' the woman said. 'Nearly took my shopping with him.'

'I should try not to worry,' Jaimie advised, smiling gently. 'Look, I really need to check you over. I think you may have cracked a rib.'

'My head hurts.'

'Yes, I'm afraid you're probably going to have a nasty headache for a while. The ambulance is on its way, and they'll soon make you feel more comfortable.'

She was able to reassure him, having made a cursory examination which, to her relief, showed no obvious signs of more serious injury. The head wound was probably going to need stitching but it wouldn't leave a scar.

She studied him more closely. He was about thirty,

she judged, and probably quite good-looking under different circumstances.

She shivered again, wishing the ambulance would get there. The man's pallor indicated that he was suffering from shock as much as from the cold. She bent to lift the pad and was checking his head wound when a distinctly male voice suddenly intruded into the silence, making her jump.

'All right, little lady. Leave that and let's have you out of there. I'll take over now.'

Startled, she half turned to find herself staring into a pair of frowning blue eyes as the man peered into the car.

'But I was—'

'Look, I know you want to help,' he said impatiently, 'but it's best if you let me get in there. I'm afraid amateurish first aid may cause more harm than good in a situation like this, so come on, be a good girl and move out of the way.'

Colour flared hotly into her cheeks as she craned her neck awkwardly to look at him.

He had to be over six feet tall. His hair was dark, almost black, dampened by snow. It would have been a handsome face, except for the compelling harshness about the features as he stared past her. She gasped as a pair of strong hands suddenly caught her round the waist in a firm grip.

'I'm sorry but I really don't have time to argue. This needs an expert so let's have you out of there before you cause any damage.'

'But you don't understand—'

'I'm sorry, young lady, but I don't have time to argue.'

Jaimie gave a yelp of surprise as she was suddenly

lifted bodily from the seat. Her fingers made contact with tautly muscled arms as he moved back slowly, taking her with him. For several seconds, it seemed as if she was suspended effortlessly in mid-air so that her body made contact with the solid wall of the man's chest as she was lifted bodily from the seat.

For a few seconds she was stunned by the power of the sensations that ran through her, then anger reasserted itself and the breath momentarily snagged in her throat as she tried to free herself, only to feel his grasp tighten.

'H-how dare you? Let me go this instant.'

For a brief moment he stared at her, taking in the pale oval of her face. She looked like a child with her hair plastered flat by the snow.

She saw him frown. Powerful shoulders moved in taut definition beneath the leather jacket he was wearing, then she let out a shrill protest as she found herself dumped unceremoniously onto her feet.

She couldn't believe it was happening as he stared past her and thrust her painfully aside as he moved to look at the man who had mercifully lapsed briefly into unconsciousness again.

'I hope you didn't attempt to move him?' he said briskly.

'No, I...I was trying to...'

'Look, be a good girl, get out of my way and don't ever try doing something like this again. It's a job for an adult, someone who knows what they're doing.' He glanced briefly at his watch. 'It's getting late. Shouldn't you be getting home? It's almost dark.'

Without giving her a chance to speak, he turned away, leaving her standing there, shaking with mingled anger and resentment.

Her mouth moved briefly on a sharp retort that she was a doctor and knew precisely what she was doing, then in the distance she heard the siren of an approaching ambulance.

Tight-lipped, she turned and almost ran to her car where she sat, blinking hard to stop the tears that pricked at her eyes.

'Good girl'! She couldn't believe he had said it. The injustice of the attack stayed with her as she finally started the engine and drove away as quickly as possible from the scene and the memory of the man who had taken charge, dismissing her as if she were a schoolgirl. How dared he?

She was still shaking when she drove towards the outskirts of the town and finally located the Felldale surgery. She sat for a moment, drawing several deep breaths in an attempt to recover her composure before going to meet the man with whom she would be working. One bad-tempered individual in a day was quite enough, she thought.

Then her ill humour vanished as she walked up the steps and into Reception. The girl behind the desk looked up, smiling. 'Hello, can I help you? You're a bit early for afternoon surgery, I'm afraid.'

'Well, actually, I was looking for Dr Paige. He is expecting me. My name is Dr Grant.'

'Jaimie, my dear!'

She turned and found herself enveloped in an embrace by her father's dearest friend. 'Uncle Jon. Oh, it's so good to see you. It's been ages.'

Jonathan Reynolds glanced at the girl behind the desk and smiled. 'It's all right, Maggie, this is Jaimie. I told you she'd be joining us at the practice. You can meet her properly later. Right now we've got some catching up to do.'

Almost before Jaimie knew it, they were sitting in the consulting room, exchanging news and enjoying a cup of coffee.

'It really is so good to see you.' Jonathan Reynolds sat in his chair, studying her. 'It's been a long time, my dear, far too long. I've heard all about your progress, of course, and I'm very proud of you. I'm even more delighted that you've agreed to come and help us out for a while.'

'It's the very least I can do.' Jaimie smiled. 'I'm not sure I would have had the courage to go into medicine at all if it hadn't been for you and Dad, you do know that?'

'Nonsense. It was in the blood. Can't argue with that.' He proffered a plate of biscuits. She shook her head and he pulled a face. 'Neither should I. They're supposed to be bad for me. *Everything's* bad for me if I listen to the experts, which I don't most of the time.'

She joined in his laughter but wasn't fooled. Her glance flickered in his direction. The change in Jonathan had shocked her, even though she was careful not to let it show as she looked at the once stout frame, now considerably thinner, and saw the tell-tale greyish tinge to his mouth. Her throat tightened.

'How long is it before you're allowed back to work—officially, that is?' she added with a smile.

He sighed and dunked a biscuit in his coffee. 'They mentioned three months. Ridiculous, of course. They're being overcautious and I told them so. Provided I take it easy, I see no reason why I can't potter around, do the odd spot of paperwork.'

He helped himself to more coffee, eyed the plate of biscuits and ruefully pushed it away. 'In the meantime...' he sat back and studied her '...I'm delighted that you're here, Jaimie. I don't feel it's fair to ask Sam to cope alone. He would do, mind. Sam's a first-class doctor. I'm lucky to have him, especially as he could have aimed for a bigger practice.'

'So why didn't he?'

'I don't really know. Partly to do with personal reasons. I didn't press the issue, probably—if I'm honest—because I was glad to have him. I did hear a rumour that he'd had a pretty bad time a couple or so years back.' He frowned. 'Not sure what happened. A girl was involved, I think. Sam didn't volunteer any information so I didn't ask. Anyway, things weren't too easy here after David Cummins left to move south.'

Jon sighed. 'The fact is, I can't ask Sam to go on indefinitely, taking normal surgeries as well as emergency calls and covering at weekends. Which is why I wrote to your dad.'

Jaimie gave him a reluctant smile. 'I'm flattered that you thought of me, Uncle Jon, but you do realise I don't have any practical experience in general practice behind me as yet? I'd hate to let you down.'

'Well, there's only one way to remedy that.' He looked at her keenly. 'I confess to a certain bias in your favour, my dear, but I do appreciate the responsibility I have to my patients. I have every confidence in your ability. And, besides, you have to start somewhere. Why not here?'

Jaimie laughed exasperatedly. 'The question is, how will Dr Paige feel about it? He, after all, is the one I'll be working with. I'll pull my weight but—'

'Sam left the decision to me. In any case, he got your letter and the mere fact that you trained at St Joseph's, *and* came out top of your group, was enough to convince him.'

Her doubts hadn't been entirely dispelled, but she managed to hide them. 'I'm looking forward to meeting him.' She glanced at her watch just as the phone rang in the adjoining office. Jon moved to answer it.

'That's probably Sam now. He wanted to fit in as many visits as he could before evening surgery. I'll show you around and introduce you to everyone.' He smiled wryly. 'At least I'm allowed to do that. Maggie can probably explain the set-up better than I can. Just let me speak to Sam—tell him you've arrived.'

Well, that should make his day, Jaimie thought as she helped herself to more coffee and glanced round the room, trying to imagine herself seeing patients in here.

She heard her own name being mentioned. It was a brief conversation and Jon's face held a worried expression as he returned to the room. 'Problems?'

'Mmm, I'm afraid so.' He frowned. 'That was Sam. I'm afraid he's going to be delayed. Something cropped up and he has to deal with it. Look, I'm sorry. It's a damned nuisance. Evening surgery starts in about half an hour.' He frowned. 'It's just as well I'm here. I think I'd better get Maggie to put everything through to me.'

Jaimie was already on her feet. 'Let me help. There must be something I can do. That's what I'm here for, after all.'

He looked at her uncertainly. 'But I haven't even

had time to show you around or introduce you to everyone.'

'I've met Maggie, sort of.' She smiled. 'Anyway, as both you and Dad have pointed out, it's sometimes best to leap straight in at the deep end.'

His look of doubt was tinged with undisguised relief. 'Well, if you're sure? Sam asked if you'd have any objections to starting the surgery. I'm sure he won't be much longer getting back.'

The feeling of panic welled up again, but she said brightly, 'Of course, I'd be happy to.' She was already reaching for her briefcase, feeling her heart thud uncomfortably in her chest. 'If someone can just point me in the right direction and show me where everything is.'

'Well, at least I can do that. Oh, and by the way, my dear, I expect your dad told you—there's a cottage for you to use for as long as you're here. David Cummins used it for a few months while he was with us. It's been kept aired so you're welcome to make use of it. You could stay with me, of course, but I thought you'd appreciate some privacy and it's more convenient for the surgery.'

'Thank you, that will be nice.' She gave a wry smile. 'Everything I brought with me is packed into a couple of suitcases and a few boxes so it won't take too long to move in.'

A quick tour of the practice was reassuring. The modern building proved to be light and airy as well as well equipped.

The waiting room was large, its walls painted in a soothing pastel shade, and Jaimie was pleased to see that there were pictures as well as some large, green plants and several tables with magazines on them.

Jon correctly interpreted her expression. 'Things have changed a bit since I first became a GP, I'm glad to say.' He opened various doors. 'This is the treatment room. We carry out a few minor ops—removal of cysts, that sort of thing. This, of course, is Reception. Maggie will show you where everything is. I don't know how we'd manage without her. She practically runs the place.'

Maggie Thomas was an attractive, dark-haired twenty-six-year-old. She grinned. 'Well, someone has to.'

He led the way along the corridor and opened another door. 'And this will be your consulting room. It's not very big, I'm afraid.'

Jaimie looked at the carpeted floor and the brightly coloured curtains which could be drawn round the examination couch. There were well-stacked bookshelves and a large desk on which stood a computer. She smiled. 'It's lovely. There's everything I need.'

'Apart from a sandwich or two,' a smiling figure announced from the doorway. Entering the room, the girl proffered the plate. 'I thought you might be glad of these, especially as a certain slave-driver is probably going to put you straight to work.'

Brown eyes twinkled as she looked at Jaimie. She was about thirty years old, of medium height and slimly built. 'I'm Ruth Dixon, practice manager and general dogsbody around here. Welcome to Felldale, Dr Grant. We're certainly glad to have you join us.'

Jon grinned. 'Anything you need, or need to know, ask Ruth. If she doesn't have the answer she'll know someone who does.'

Jaimie laughed as her hand was clasped in a warm,

friendly grip. 'I'm afraid I may take up rather a lot
of your time, just until I find my way around.'

'Don't worry about it—that's what I'm here for.'
Ruth looked at her watch. 'I'd better leave you to it.
Surgery starts in about ten minutes and it's already
fairly busy out there. Don't forget, if there's a problem just call.'

Jaimie crossed to the desk and put her briefcase
down. 'Well, I suppose I'd better make a start.' She
switched on the computer and was shocked to find
that her hands were shaking. 'I do hope I'm not going
to let you down, Uncle Jon.'

He patted her hand. 'You're going to be just fine.
The folk around here are nice and friendly.' His eyes
twinkled. 'Some of them are in for a bit of a surprise
when they come through that door.' He chuckled.
'Come to think of it, Sam may be in for a bit of a
shock, too.'

He was gone before she could ask him why Sam
Paige would be surprised and then Maggie Thomas
brought in the first batch of patients' cards and she
promptly forgot about it completely as the first patient
walked in.

All in all it turned out to be less of an ordeal than
she had imagined, and the time passed remarkably
quickly. There was a slipped disc and the almost inevitable batch of sore throats, followed by a young
woman who ushered a fractious five-year-old boy into
the room.

Jaimie invited the woman to sit down and the five-
year-old promptly climbed onto his mother's knee
and began to investigate the pocket of her coat.

'Don't do that, Peter. I told you, no more chocolates.' She looked warily at Jaimie. 'I thought we were going to see Dr Paige. We always see Dr Paige.'

Jaimie smiled what she hoped was a reassuring smile. 'Yes, I'm sorry about that. Unfortunately Dr Paige has been delayed slightly, and as I shall be joining the practice anyway on a temporary basis until Dr Reynolds is back at work I stepped in at the last minute. So, what can I do for you?'

'It's young Peter. He's had a cold for about a week now and he says his ears hurt. It's driving me mad, Doctor, what with trying to keep him occupied. And he's off his food. It's not like him. He's usually such a good eater.'

Jaimie retrieved a box of tissues from a sticky hand and smiled. 'It won't do him any harm not to eat for a while, Mrs Morgan, as long as he has plenty of fluids.'

'He won't drink milk.'

'If he prefers flavoured drinks to milk or water, I'd let him have them for a while, provided you avoid the ones with a high sugar content. Let's have a look at you, shall we, young man?'

It didn't really need an examination to tell her that the child was suffering from a mild ear infection brought on by a heavy cold, but she made the usual careful examination. She checked the child's ears and throat, listening to his chest and feeling his neck for raised glands.

'Well, he's not too bad. His ears are slightly pink and his glands are up a bit so he's probably feeling quite grotty, aren't you, poor little chap?'

She ruffled the child's hair. 'I'm going to give you a prescription for an antibiotic. Make sure he finishes the course, even if after a few days you think he's much better. You can give him Calpol. It will help to keep his temperature down and generally make him feel a bit better.'

She tapped out a prescription. 'I'm sure you'll see a marked improvement over the next couple of days. If not, or you're at all worried, please, come back and see me—or Dr Paige—again.'

Sue Morgan got to her feet, clutching the prescription with a smile of relief. Smiling, Jaimie saw her out.

She worked solidly for two hours and she was just congratulating herself on having survived the ordeal relatively unscathed when the door opened again.

Having been told that the last patient had gone, Jaimie did a hasty recount of her patients' cards and assumed, without looking up, that it was simply a late arrival.

Completing the notes she was making, she smiled. 'Hello, do sit down. I'll be with you in a moment.'

She heard the sharp hiss of indrawn breath then an angry voice said, 'What the hell is going on here? Perhaps you'd be kind enough to explain who you are and what the devil you're doing behind that desk?'

He spoke in a tightly controlled voice as Jaimie looked directly into the darkly sombre eyes that regarded her with such open and unjustified hostility.

Shock brought her slowly, unsteadily, to her feet. It wasn't possible. But as her gaze rose agonisingly, she was once again conscious of steely blue eyes set in chiselled features, and premonition slowly became reality.

'You!' The word seemed to have been forced from his lips.

She swallowed hard, telling herself even now that

it must all be some terrible mistake as she forced herself to face him.

But it was no mistake. It was *him*, the man who had manhandled her, who had dared to accuse her of putting an injured man's life at risk with her amateurish first aid.

His jaw clenched perceptibly as he considered her briefly from beneath ridiculously thick lashes. 'I'm waiting for an explanation, young lady, and it had better be good.'

She watched him warily. 'I might say the same thing,' she said tetchily. She didn't know this man from Adam. He had simply walked in, unannounced. He could be *anyone*.

However, she noticed that even though his jeans were faded they were of good quality. The fact should have reassured her but it didn't. He managed to look at the same time both faintly disreputable and very dangerously male, and his unannounced presence in the small room was beginning to have a definitely unsettling effect on her nervous system.

His gaze narrowed. 'I'd strongly advise you not to play games with me. You could find yourself in serious trouble.'

She didn't doubt it. Powerful shoulders moved as he slowly eased down the zip of his black leather jacket.

Jaimie swallowed hard. 'If you must know, I'm here as locum to Dr Paige until Dr Reynolds is well enough to return to work after his heart attack.' She resented the look of disbelief on his face.

'Is this someone's idea of a joke? I'm Dr Paige.'

Her chin rose. 'Then you must have been expecting me. Surely Jon must have told you...?'

'I was expecting a Dr Grant.'

'That's right. *I'm* Dr Grant.'

He gave a short laugh of disbelief. 'Why the hell didn't you say something when we met earlier?'

She ran a hand through her hair in a gesture of exasperation. 'Because you hardly gave me the chance. You were so eager to take charge.'

'Can you blame me? You looked like a child.'

'Well, obviously I'm not.'

'I can see that—now.'

Jaimie felt her colour deepen as his gaze raked her appearance from the top of her chestnut hair, lingering over the fullness of her breasts and the slender curve of her hips.

'And you're obviously not Dr *James* Grant.'

'Obviously not.' She felt a stab of resentment. 'Look, Jon must have talked to you.'

'Vaguely. He wanted to bring someone in. I told him I could cope.'

'Obviously he felt you shouldn't have to.'

His gaze narrowed. 'You signed your letter as Dr James Grant.'

'I can hardly be held responsible if you misread the signature,' she said snappily. 'I imagine if you'd shown any real interest Uncle Jon would have told you.'

She gave a sigh of exasperation. She was rapidly coming to the conclusion that she would never be able to work with a man like Sam Paige. It had all been a terrible mistake and it was all too clear that he shared her view.

CHAPTER TWO

'THIS isn't going to work, is it?'

'Probably not.' Jaimie had to fight a sudden desire to collect her briefcase and jacket and walk out there and then, except that she had absolutely no intention of being intimidated by Sam Paige.

His mere presence seemed to fill the room. Studying him more closely, she realised that he was taller than she had first imagined. As he half sat, half stood against the desk she decided that he was quite attractive in a rugged sort of way. Not that he was her type, of course, but she could see why some women would fall for the dark good looks.

In the street there had been no time to notice the tiny lines of tiredness around his mouth, but they were there, adding a kind of harshness which left her feeling vaguely shaky.

Her gaze shifted quickly to his eyes. They were shadowed, a reminder, if one were needed, of the workload he had been carrying since Uncle Jon's heart attack. Having dealt with only one surgery, she could suddenly understand why.

She drew a deep, steadying breath. 'So, what are we going to do?'

'God knows.' He ruffled a hand through his hair. 'It's a damned mess. There's obviously been some mistake.' He threw his jacket onto the chair where she had been sitting and she stiffened at the proprietorial gesture.

28

'I don't see that there has been a mistake. I understood that you required a locum. I'm it. I'm here and I'm willing to work.'

He gave a slight laugh. 'I don't think you have any idea of what you'll be taking on here.'

'Maybe not, yet. But I'm willing to learn, and may I remind you that I am a fully qualified doctor?'

'Newly qualified.'

Her lips tightened. 'But qualified nonetheless.'

Sam Paige straightened up and dug his hands into his pockets, staring at her with the kind of speculation that made her feel oddly vulnerable.

'This is a busy rural practice, Doctor, and it's best you understand now that I don't have time to act as nursemaid to you while you find your way around. Our patients are scattered over a wide area. In summer we get the tourists.'

'So you said in your letter. I'm not afraid of a challenge.'

He gave a wry smile. 'Well, I can certainly promise you it will be that. I just hope you don't imagine the job will be a sinecure. I'm afraid we have very little to offer in the way of excitement here in Felldale.'

'I dare say I'll survive, somehow.' Stung by the element of scorn in his voice, Jaimie flicked him a glance and felt her throat tighten for a few seconds as she became aware of those shrewd blue eyes running over her.

'Just how old did you say you were, Dr Grant?'

'I didn't. But if you feel you must know, I'm twenty-five, nearly twenty-six.'

Surprise flickered briefly over his features. 'You look about eighteen.'

'So I've been told, but I can hardly help that.'

Blue eyes glinted. 'It's hardly likely to instil confidence in the patients when they walk in here and see you sitting behind that desk.'

'I seem to have managed reasonably well so far.' She stabbed a finger at the pile of cards on the desk. 'I coped with a full list of patients and no one complained.' That wasn't exactly true. After an hour she had resigned herself to the wary looks that greeted her as each new patient walked in.

But Sam Paige's gaze barely passed over the cards. 'Unfortunately, one surgery hardly qualifies you as an expert.' He frowned then bent to shuffle through the pile. 'I was supposed to see Mrs Prentiss this evening.'

Jaimie frowned. 'Prentiss. Oh, yes, I remember. She came in.'

He looked from her to the card, scanning the details she had written, then his eyes narrowed. 'You've changed her treatment.'

'That's right. I judged it to be the appropriate action to take.'

'On what grounds?'

Jaimie frowned as, for a moment, her confidence faltered, only to be replaced by certainty in her judgement. 'We had a long chat.'

'She has a history of coughs and sore throats. I last saw her about five months ago.'

Jaimie nodded. 'The pattern is pretty much the same. I examined her. Her throat was red and her glands were a bit swollen.'

'That sounds familiar.' He looked at her. 'But you decided not to prescribe antibiotics.'

'Yes, I did.'

He laughed and it was a surprisingly pleasant sound. 'I bet that went down well.'

Jaimie smiled wryly. 'She wasn't too happy about it but, as I explained, antibiotics aren't always the answer and they can sometimes produce problems in themselves—like thrush, for instance, or diarrhoea. At worse, in rare cases, I explained that some patients have an allergic reaction, possibly life-threatening, to certain antibiotics. So, finally, we agreed she would go home and rest, take aspirin to relieve the discomfort and see how it went.'

Sam Paige grunted. 'I agree with the theory. It may not work.'

'Maybe not, but it was worth a try. I suggested she make an appointment for next week and told her that, in the meantime, if she feels she isn't making progress, she should come back to the surgery.'

He tossed the card back on to the desk and ruffled a hand through his hair. 'Well, you obviously did all the right things, but don't let it go to your head, Doctor. One surgery isn't general practice.'

'I realise that.'

'I wonder if you do.' He crossed to the window, staring out into the darkness which had somehow crept in unnoticed as she worked. 'Everything's changing. You've seen what it's like around here. It's green, we have the hills and open fields, but gradually it's being swallowed up by new developments. They're building houses, new roads.'

She gave a slight smile. 'I think they call it progress.'

'Do they?' He turned to look at her. 'Well, we're the ones who have to bear the brunt of that progress, Dr Grant, and I just hope you're up to it because, believe me, the novelty factor soon wears thin. It's no joke, being called out of your bed in the middle of the night in winter, sometimes for nothing more than a dose of indigestion. Crowded surgeries aren't fun.'

'I did realise that when I decided to become a doctor. It's what I chose to do,' she added defensively.

'So did Jon Reynolds. Medicine is his life and look what it's done to him.'

Jaimie frowned. 'Aren't you forgetting something? Jon is sixty-three. I'm not saying he's had an easy life—far from it. He's always worked too hard. That's the way he is.'

She flicked him a glance and felt a slight tremor run through her, triggered by an emotion she chose not to analyse. There was something about Sam Paige which made her feel unsettled.

She sighed. 'Look, I'm not here to take Jon's place. I know I could never do that. I just want to help out for a few weeks, that's all I'm asking. Don't you at least owe me that now that I'm here? After all, it's hardly my fault that you mistook me for a man.'

For a second Jaimie stood, unmoving, as Sam Paige's gaze swept with slow appreciation over her body, taking in the jeans and sweater. Its deep jade colour suited her, but suddenly she was aware that it clung to her figure, emphasising her curves.

His blue eyes glinted briefly with humour. 'I'm not likely to make that mistake again.'

Involuntarily she tugged at her sweater in a jerky movement, but his expression had already changed and his tone was cool. 'It doesn't look as if I have any choice but to let you stay now that you're here. Unfortunately, Jon is right. I just didn't want to admit that if I'm going to do my job properly I do need help, as much to put his mind at rest as anything else.'

She swallowed hard. 'Just how bad is he?'

'Not good. It was a severe attack and not the first. He'd had an earlier warning episode.' His mouth tightened. 'The trouble is he's too conscientious. You know Jon. If he thinks his patients are getting anything less than two hundred per cent in his absence, he'll be back at his desk and probably dead within a month.'

Jaimie felt a surprising stab of pity. Whatever she personally might think of Sam Paige, she guessed that if he was hard on others he was equally hard on himself.

'All the more reason to let me share some of the burden. I can at least take some of the night calls and visits.'

'Oh, I can promise you, Dr Grant, that if you choose to stay there won't be any half-measures.' His mouth twisted. 'I give you a week, maybe two at most, and don't say I didn't warn you when you have to admit you can't take the pressure. You want to know what general practice is all about. Well, you're about to find out the hard way and we'll soon see if you're up to it.'

Jaimie drew herself up, well aware of the mockery in his eyes, yet at the same time a feeling of relief swept over her.

She was staying and she would prove to Sam Paige that she was up to the job. Somehow she would dispel his doubts about her, and if he could survive the next three months, so would she.

Jaimie hauled her briefcase from the passenger seat of her car, slammed the door and locked it, before hurrying to the back door of the surgery.

Once inside, a steady hum of noise, interspersed with the seemingly constant ringing of a telephone, told her that they were in for a busy morning.

Taking a deep breath, she headed for Reception, telling herself that the fluttering in her stomach was indigestion and not nerves. Her cheeks were flushed and she paused briefly to rest her frozen hands on the radiator.

'Hi.' The girl behind the desk greeted her arrival with a smile. 'You're nice and early. I'm Paula, by the way, junior receptionist and general girl Friday.'

'Hi. Look, I'm sorry I'm late.'

'Oh, you're not.' The girl glanced, smiling at the clock. 'Don't let the crowd out there fool you. They always like to arrive early, especially on Tuesdays.'

'What's so special about Tuesdays?'

Paula Andrews eyed her with amusement. 'It just happens to be market day. Most of them like to kill two birds with one stone—catch the early bus, pop into the surgery and then do the shopping.'

Jaimie grinned. 'Ah, I see. I'm afraid it's going to take me a while to learn the system.'

Maggie Thomas came through to Reception with a large batch of mail. She viewed Jaimie's arrival with obvious surprise and relief.

'Hello, Doctor. This is a nice surprise. We didn't expect you in on your first morning. You can't have had time to settle in yet.'

'It doesn't take long to unpack a couple of suit-cases.' Jaimie smiled. 'I'm glad I packed my winter woollies, mind you. I think I'm definitely going to need time to acclimatise.'

Maggie laughed. 'I've lived here for ten years and every year the amount of snow still takes me by surprise.' She dropped the mail on to the desk. 'Seriously, though, Dr Paige didn't mention that you'd be in today. I'm sure he wasn't expecting you, but I, for one, am certainly glad to see you.'

No, he wouldn't have mentioned it, Jaimie thought. He was probably hoping she'd have turned tail and run in the night. Well, she wasn't about to give him that satisfaction.

'I'm afraid I was a bit late getting here. I had to de-ice the car.'

'Don't worry about it.'

'Not exactly the best of starts, though, is it?' She glanced at her watch. 'I suppose Dr Paige is in already?'

'About half an hour ago.'

Of course, he would be. Mr Perfect. Jaimie sighed. 'Well, in that case, judging by the crowd out there, the sooner I also get started the better.'

Maggie eyed her with amusement. 'Oh, a lot of that will be the curiosity factor. You'd be surprised how quickly word gets around in a small place like this. They'll all be wanting to take a look at the new lady doctor.'

'Oh, dear. In that case, I'd better not disappoint them.'

'You'll be needing these.' Maggie handed over a batch of cards, smiling as a young man, holding a small child by the hand, approached the desk. 'Morning, Mr Harris. It's young Ben, is it? Take a seat. Doctor will be with you in a few minutes.'

Jaimie made her way to her consulting room, taking a few seconds to run a comb through her hair before pressing the bell to summon her first patient.

Her cheeks were still flushed from the cold wind, adding emphasis to her blue eyes. The thick mane of naturally wavy chestnut hair was swept back and she applied a touch of lipstick to her full, soft mouth. Her gaze travelled briefly over the bronze-coloured silk shirt and the neatly tailored, knee-length skirt before she moved to the desk and rang the bell.

All in all the time passed remarkably quickly, with the usual batch of verrucas, sore throats and back-aches, most of which could be treated with soluble aspirins, though a few needed antibiotics to clear persistent infections.

Jaimie looked up, smiling, as the last of her patients, an elderly figure muffled in coat, scarf and cap, edged his way round the door, eyeing her suspiciously.

She motioned the hobbling figure to a chair beside her desk. 'Mr Travers. Please, make yourself comfortable and tell me what I can do for you.'

'I was expecting to see Dr Reynolds. I always see Dr Reynolds or Dr Paige.'

Jaimie hid a smile. 'Yes, I'm sorry about that. Unfortunately Dr Reynolds is ill and I'm here to help lessen Dr Paige's workload a little.'

She felt her heart sink. This was the first patient who had actually shown any reluctance to consult her and it was disconcerting. The wary glances she had expected and been ready for, but this was something else. Suppose they all started insisting on seeing Sam.

She smiled what she hoped was a reassuring smile. 'I know Dr Paige is a little busy right now. Perhaps I can help? If you feel you need to see a doctor again you'll be able to make an appointment to see Dr Paige in a few days' time.'

Charlie Travers grunted unhappily but ventured further into the room. Seen closer to, she judged his age to be about seventy.

'You look very uncomfortable.' She smiled. 'How long has that foot been bothering you?'

'It's been a couple of weeks now. Damn thing.'

'Mmm. Look, why don't you slip your shoe and sock off so that I can take a look.'

Jaimie made a careful examination of the obviously swollen foot and heard his sharp intake of breath as she gently pressed the side of his big toe. 'Yes, I see. It must be very painful.'

'Well, it don't help when you poke it, that's for sure.' He grunted. 'Had the devil of a job getting my shoe on this morning.'

Jaimie nodded. 'Yes, I can see, it's quite swollen. It feels hot, too. All right, Mr Travers, you can pop your shoe back on now.' She straightened up, entering a few notes onto the computer before looking at him. 'Well, what you've got, Mr Travers, is gout.'

'Gout! Nay, never.' Charlie was horrified. 'I'm tee-total, as near as dammit. At most I might sup a glass of ale. I never touch—'

'Mr Travers, I believe you.' Jaimie smiled. 'Gout has nothing to do with the amount of alcohol you drink. That's an old wives' tale.'

'What? You mean...'

'Anyone can get gout. It's caused by a build-up of something called uric acid crystals in a joint, in this case your big toe.'

Charlie Travers looked relieved. 'Aye, well, it's just as well. If word got around as I'd been supping on the quiet, I'd never be able to hold my head up in church of a Sunday morning.' He looked at her. 'So what are you going to do about it?'

'I'll give you some tablets.' Jaimie tapped out the prescription, waited as it printed out, tore it off and signed it, before handing it to him. 'These should do the trick in no time. Take three a day, and if you get any more problems come and see me—or Dr Paige— any time.'

Smiling, she watched him hobble out, and with a small sigh she made her way to the small staffroom where Maggie was making coffee. The waiting room was empty and she was pleased to see there was no sign of Sam.

'I bet you're ready for this.' Maggie proffered a cup. 'Help yourself to sugar. We had some biscuits somewhere but someone seems to have scoffed the lot.' She grinned. 'I can't imagine who. Help yourself to milk and sugar.'

'I hadn't realised how much I needed this until now. Mmm, that tastes good.'

Maggie sipped at her own coffee. 'So, how did it go?'

'It wasn't quite as nerve-racking as I expected.' Jaimie smiled wryly as she spooned sugar into her cup. 'I'm not sure how the patients felt about it. Old Mr Travers certainly wasn't too happy about having a new doctor foisted on him. I suspect the fact that it was a lady doctor probably added insult to injury.'

Maggie gave a hoot of laughter. 'Oh, don't take any notice of Charlie. He loves a good grumble. If it wasn't that it would be something else. He's all right really.'

'Yes, I realised that.' Jaimie sank into a chair with

a sigh of relief. 'Anyway, he seemed happy enough when he left.'

She sipped at her coffee. 'Medicine is such a personal business, isn't it? People get used to their doctor. They build up a relationship which involves a certain amount of trust. They don't like change. Not that I'm going to be here long enough for them to get used to me.'

She frowned, wondering why the thought should give her a sense of disappointment, then pulled herself up sharply, telling herself there was no point getting attached to things, or people.

The door opened and the likelihood vanished as Sam Paige's frowning glance raked her as she sat in the chair.

She found herself battling against a feeling of guilt, which was ridiculous because she had put in a good morning's work. She swallowed a mouthful of too-hot coffee, feeling it burn her throat as the cup rattled into the saucer.

Purposely, she forced herself to relax, ignoring him as she bent her head over the medical journal she picked up from the table.

'I take it that's the lot?' Still frowning, he eyed the coffee-pot.

'Unless we're hiding some somewhere.' Maggie's voice held a note of humour as she glanced in Jaimie's direction. 'It wasn't as bad as I thought it might be, thanks to Dr Grant. Here's your coffee, Doctor. Sorry we're out of biscuits.' She handed him the cup.

He took it, glancing at his watch. 'I don't really have time for this. How many visits are there?'

'Half a dozen, including Dan Burrows. He's run

out of his usual arthritis tablets. I said you'd pop in to see him.'

Sam grunted, scanning the list as he drank his coffee. 'Hmm, I suppose it's not too bad. Three look pretty routine. I'd better call in on Dan first. I'm not too happy about him. His arthritis is getting to the point where we're going to have to get him into hospital to get those knee joints done.'

'Do you think you'll be able to persuade him?' Maggie's smile was resigned. 'You know how he feels about hospitals.'

'I don't think he's going to have much choice. He's on the strongest dose of painkillers I can give him. They're beginning to upset his stomach and the pain must be pretty near unbearable, even if he won't admit it.'

'He misses his wife.'

'I know.' Sam put his cup down. Maggie gathered them up and took them away and Jaimie found herself waiting, illogically frustrated, for some sign that he had noticed her. When it seemed it wasn't to be forthcoming she rose to her feet.

'I'm sorry I was late in this morning,' she said carefully. 'It won't happen again.' She gave a slight laugh in an attempt to lighten the atmosphere. 'I had to de-ice the car. I forgot winter lasts a little longer here than down south.'

His gaze moved from the list to her face. 'It's not a problem. I didn't expect you to take a surgery this morning anyway.'

She gave a short laugh of exasperation. 'Why not? I thought I'd made it perfectly clear last night that I'm here to do a job and I fully intend to pull my weight.'

'I'm glad to hear it.' His eyes skimmed sardonically over her and she felt her colour deepen as the coolly brooding gaze subjected her to a flagrantly masculine appraisal that took her breath away. 'The question is, are you up to it?'

'Oh, come on.' She gave a short laugh. 'I thought we'd been over this. I'm tougher than I look. Isn't your attitude just a little old-fashioned, Dr Paige?'

'My attitude, as you put it, has nothing to do with it. I'm a realist. I can't afford to be anything else. The welfare of my patients depends on my ability to do my job, and the truth is that I don't have time to worry about whether you can cope.'

She drew in a breath but refused to be drawn. Her chin rose. 'I can take care of myself. It may surprise you to know that I can even read a map.'

'Really?' He laughed aloud. 'Then you must be one of the few women I know who can.'

Jaimie's gaze flew up to meet his and found his eyes regarding her with mocking amusement. Her cheeks flamed. 'Look, I really do want to help. I've been studying a map of the local area. Once I know the addresses I can look them up. In any case, I do have a tongue in my head.'

'Now, that I don't doubt.'

She wasn't sure whether it was sarcasm or laughter that filled his eyes but she felt her temper rise.

'This is ridiculous. It certainly isn't getting us anywhere. I want to help, but it seems your mind is made up so there's no point in arguing...'

Dismissively she started to walk away. His hand shot out, swinging her to face him. His touch had a totally illogical effect on her. She was suddenly conscious of a crazy vortex of emotions that surged over her like a huge tidal wave, leaving her feeling dazed and bewildered.

She stared up at him, bemused. The blue eyes returned her gaze steadily and she saw his mouth curve in silent laughter.

'Are you always this fiery?'

'Only when provoked.' Furiously she tried to free her arm, but his grasp merely tightened, drawing her closer.

'I do seem to bring out the worst in you, don't I?' he said evenly. 'I'm not saying I'm not grateful.'

'I don't want your gratitude, Doctor,' Jaimie said heatedly. 'All I'm asking is that you let me do my share. Judge me on results, not on your own obvious prejudices. Forget I'm a woman.'

'That might be rather difficult.'

'Well, do your best,' she snapped, and then she realised that he was laughing at her. Her mouth twisted. 'Look, I know you don't want me here, but now that I am don't you think it will be better for both of us if we try to accept the situation and make the best of it? After all, it's only likely to be for a few weeks. I think I can just about cope with that if you can.'

He stood, looking at her, and she was suddenly uncomfortably aware of him as a man, an attractive man at that.

He frowned. 'As far as Jon is concerned, it will only be a few weeks.'

Jaimie stared at him. 'I don't understand. Surely you're not saying…?'

'I'm saying that Jon has made his mind up. He believes what he wants to believe. He's convinced himself that he's going to get back to work.'

'And…are you saying that he won't?' She felt a cold stab of fear.

'I'm saying that he's more ill than he chooses to realise.'

For a moment Jaimie was bereft of speech. She moistened her dry lips with her tongue. 'But I thought… He said he was over the heart attack. He seemed so well when I spoke to him.'

'I don't doubt it. He knew you were coming. Perhaps you should reserve judgement until you've seen him when he's tired or you catch him off guard.'

Jaimie stared at the other doctor bleakly. She swallowed hard. 'So just how bad is he?' When he didn't answer she went on, 'I have a right to know. He and my father have been friends for years. They go way back. He's always been like a real uncle to me.'

A spasm flickered across Sam's features, leaving them taut. 'It's not good. The attack was worse than he realises, and he could have another at any time.'

Jaimie moistened her dry lips with her tongue. 'And you're saying he doesn't know?'

'If he does he's not letting on.' His gaze levelled with hers. 'Don't you see? Jon's work is his life. Take it away and he may as well be dead as far as he's concerned.' He frowned. 'Why do you think when he started talking about bringing in a locum that I tried to play it down?'

Jaimie stared at him uneasily. 'There was no way you could go on carrying the workload alone. You must have known that.'

'I would have managed somehow.'

'What made you change your mind?'

'I didn't.' His mouth twisted. 'I gave in because

Jon had convinced himself that it really would only be for a few weeks.'

'And now you're saying that isn't true?'

'Do you want me to be honest or shall I wrap it up nicely for you?'

'Just tell me the truth. What exactly is the prognosis?'

He looked at her and drew a deep breath. 'Basically, I'd say it stinks. But you're a doctor. I'm sure you can work it out for yourself.'

He was right. She just didn't want to have to put it into words. But how could she insist in one breath that she was capable of doing her job if she was going to go to pieces at the first hurdle?

She straightened her shoulders and looked at him. 'All right. What if he doesn't go back to work? What if he takes things easy?'

Sam gave a short laugh. 'It's a nice idea. You think you can persuade him? Go ahead. I've tried.' His face was grim as he bent to pick up the case notes Maggie had left on the table. 'Chances are he could go on for several years. But Jon isn't the sort to sit back and let others do the work—you must know that.'

'So what do we do?'

'There's nothing we can do, except carry on. It's out of our hands. One way or another, Jon will eventually come to terms with it.'

She frowned. 'Wouldn't it be kinder to tell him the truth?'

He gave a slight laugh. 'Do you want to be the one to do it?'

'No.' She swallowed hard. 'I suppose I don't.'

'No, it's not that easy, is it?'

But she wasn't going to be put off. 'You and I

arguing isn't going to solve anything is it? I know you resent me, but I'm here—'

'And I'd better learn to put up with you?'

Jaimie drew herself up and faced him. 'I care for Jon, too. Very much, as it happens, and I intend doing what I can to help, whether you like it or not. I'm just not sure what I have to do to prove to you that I'm capable.'

'I'm not asking you to prove anything.'

'Aren't you?' Her voice shook. 'Then perhaps it's me, as a woman, that you object to. Well, I'm sorry, there's not a lot I can do about that, but I will pull my weight, starting with taking a share of those calls.' She held out her hand.

There was a momentary pause then he drew three cards out of the pile, tossing them onto the table in front of her.

'If there's one thing I can't abide, it's a bossy woman.'

In spite of herself she laughed. 'You'd better get used to it because I'm here and I'm staying.'

His gaze narrowed briefly. Somehow, almost without her noticing, he had moved closer. 'One of these days, Dr Grant,' he said huskily, 'someone is going to teach you a lesson, and it might come as something of a shock.'

She choked. 'And if there's one thing I can't stand it's arrogant, self-opinionated—' She stifled the rest as the door opened and Paula Andrews beamed round the door.

'Oh, Dr Paige, there was a telephone call for you. You weren't in your room so I took a message. Miss Forbes called and said she'll expect you for dinner at eight this evening.'

Jaimie felt the colour deepen in her cheeks. She was briefly aware of his mocking stare as she backed away, gathered up the case notes and marched briskly out of the room.

It was galling to find herself wondering just who the mysterious Miss Forbes was. Probably large, tweedy and seventy if she was a day. 'Just his type,' she muttered uncharitably.

But somehow the image she had conjured up didn't seem to fit, and for some illogical reason the knowledge rankled. She found herself wondering briefly about the other woman in his life, the one Uncle Jon had mentioned. Sam obviously believed there was safety in numbers, she thought, and who could argue with that?

She pushed the thoughts firmly aside as she climbed into her car. She wasn't in the least bit interested in Sam Paige or his love life. She was here to work and she would do it, with or without his co-operation.

The gears grated noisily and Jaimie swore softly under her breath as she drove away, all too aware of the tall figure standing at the window, no doubt laughing his male chauvinist head off.

CHAPTER THREE

JAIMIE winced as the car wheel hit another rut in the uneven country lane. Light drizzle had gradually turned into a downpour and she flicked on the windscreen wipers, leaning forward to peer into the murkiness ahead.

'I'll bet he's done this on purpose,' she thought, grimly manoeuvring the car between overhanging hedgerows. Whether by accident or design—and from the little she already knew of Sam Paige it was probably the latter—she seemed to be driving round in circles, looking for a farm which didn't appear to exist except in someone's imagination.

Reaching for the list from the seat beside her, she held it against the steering-wheel, studying it briefly as she drove. 'Bradwell Farm. Well, it's on the map so I know you're out there somewhere.'

She glanced at her watch and frowned. According to her notes, Jim Penrose was fifty-five years old and complaining of nausea and chest pains.

'Come on!' she ground out, trying to force extra speed out of the car. 'At this rate the patient will have expired before I get there and then Mr Nice Guy Paige will really have a field day.'

She rubbed a hand against the windscreen in an attempt to clear it. With a sigh of relief she spotted a turning and, swinging the wheel, a minute later she was driving into a muddy yard.

Bringing the car to a halt, she dragged her wellingtons from the back seat, slipping her feet into them before making her way precariously across the muddy yard towards the stone-built house.

A tantalising smell of frying bacon followed her across the yard. Her own breakfast had been a hastily grabbed cup of coffee and now she was beginning to regret it as her stomach gave a loud rumble.

The door was opened by a stocky woman of about fifty just as she reached it.

'Doctor.' Dora Penrose's face relaxed into a smile. 'I thought it was the farm-hands, wanting their breakfast. Come in, do. You're just in time for a nice cup of tea.'

A raw wind blew in across the fields and Jaimie gasped with relief as she followed the woman into the house.

'I'm sorry it took me a while to get here,' she explained, breathlessly, as she mopped her wet face with a handkerchief. 'I must have missed the turning about half a mile back.'

'Lor, bless you, don't you worry about that.' Dora Penrose laughed. 'You're not the first and I dare say you won't be the last. It happens all the time. Now then, let me get you that tea and a nice piece of bacon, maybe.'

Jaimie frowned. This was not a woman who appeared to be overly anxious about her husband's health. 'Er, no, thank you, really. It's very kind of you but I really think I should see Mr Penrose.' She glanced anxiously at the stairs. She was already heading in that direction, fumbling in her briefcase for her stethoscope. 'I take it he's in bed?'

'In bed! Bless you, no. He's in the kitchen.'

Jaimie paused and turned slowly. 'The kitchen?

But—' She broke off, feeling as if she had somehow, mistakenly, managed to step into a bad dream. 'Mrs Penrose, you did telephone the surgery to say that Mr Penrose was having chest pains and generally feeling unwell?'

'Aye, that's right. In awful pain he was.'

Jaimie had a sudden and all too vivid mental image of the recently expired Jim Penrose stretched out on the kitchen floor. Perhaps his wife was in shock. People dealt with shock in different ways.

'I think I'd better take a look at him straight away.'

'He'll be right glad to see you.'

Not quite expired yet then, Jaimie thought, battling with a sudden feeling of panic. How long would it take to get an ambulance along that narrow farm track, even supposing it could make it at all?

'Here we are, then. Come in, Doctor.' Mrs Penrose's ample figure led the way into the kitchen. 'Jim, it's the doctor. A nice *lady* doctor.' She chuckled. 'So you mind your manners now.'

'Mr Pen—' Jaimie came to an abrupt halt at the sight of fifty-five-year-old, stout and ruddy-complexioned Jim Penrose, seated at the kitchen table, as large as life and tucking into a hearty breakfast.

'Morning, Doctor.' He paused briefly in the act of helping himself to another sausage. 'I hope you brought a bottle of my usual indigestion mixture with you.'

Jaimie stared at him in disbelief. 'Mr Penrose…'

'I don't want no more of them pills.' His jaw jutted aggressively as he set down his knife and fork and fumbled in his pocket to produce a bottle which he dropped onto the table in front of her. 'Useless they are, useless. I took one.'

'That's right, he did.' Dora Penrose added her voice to the conversation. 'Didn't do a thing.'

'Sweeties, that's what they are. Peppermint sweeties. Fat lot of good that is when I got the gut ache.'

Jaimie felt her temper rising. 'Mr Penrose, I understood that you were complaining of chest pains and nausea.'

'Aye, that's right.' He pushed his plate towards his wife. 'I'll have another piece of that bacon, Dora, and some of that fried bread.' He looked at Jaimie. 'I got the pain and the nausea, and constipation. I'm a sick man. I should be in hospital. I told that there young doctor so, didn't I, Dora?'

'Aye, so he did.'

Jaimie drew a deep breath. 'Mr Penrose, I can assure you that if Dr Paige thought for one moment that you had anything more serious than indigestion he would have sent you to hospital for the necessary tests.' She glanced at her notes. 'I see from these that he recommended that you try to cut down on the amount of fat in your diet and that you include more fibre, things like cereals.'

'You can't expect a man to live on rubbish like that. I'm a working man. Three good, solid meals a day.' His fist thumped the table. 'That's how my dad were brought up and his dad before him, and if it was good enough for them it's good enough for me.'

'In that case, I really see no point in prescribing more medicine.' Jaimie met his look directly. 'You said yourself, it does no good.'

Jim Penrose shuffled uncomfortably in his chair and gazed down at the replenished plate in front of him. 'You can't expect a man to do a full day's work, in all weathers, without a bit of meat on his bones.'

Jaimie bit back a sigh of exasperation. 'You do realise that if you go on as you are, you run a very real risk of having a heart attack, Mr Penrose. Have you thought about what that will do to your family? What would happen to the farm if you weren't here to keep things going?'

He looked shamefaced and she guessed that he hadn't even considered the implications.

'Look, why don't I arrange for you to have a chat with our practice nurse? She's very understanding. She'll be able to work out a sensible diet with you.'

'A man can't live on a few lettuce leaves.'

'Dieting doesn't mean going hungry, Mr Penrose. It's a question of eating sensibly, substituting fruit and vegetables for fat. If you talk to the nurse she'll be able to come up with suggestions that mean you won't have to feel hungry. So, what do you say?'

His disgruntled gaze settled again on the plate. 'Aye, well, a chat maybe. No promises, mind.'

As she made her way back to her car Jaimie wondered whether he would think about what she had said and try to change his ways. Somehow, she didn't hold out too much hope.

Her next call was to a fractious two-year-old with a nasty throat infection. She left a prescription for antibiotics with the anxious mother, before heading for her final call of the morning.

It was an hour later and the afternoon light was rapidly fading when she finally returned to her car and flung her briefcase onto the back seat. She groaned as her mobile phone rang.

'Yes, Dr Grant.'

'Oh, Doctor.' Maggie Thomas sounded anxious. 'I'm glad I caught you. We've just had a call from the police, asking for urgent medical attendance. I've been trying to contact Dr Paige for the last fifteen minutes but he isn't answering his mobile.'

Jaimie's response was instantly totally professional. Visions of a warming cup of coffee were banished. 'All right, Maggie, I'll take it. Give me what details you've got.'

'It's Ted Hargreaves. He's elderly, lives on his own.'

'Do we have any idea what the problem is?'

'Only that the neighbours became concerned when they hadn't seen him around. They went round to see if he was all right and found him on the floor so they called the police. I gather he has a nasty head wound.'

Jaimie had already switched on the ignition. 'Right, Maggie, I'm on my way.'

It was starting to freeze by the time she arrived at Ted Hargreaves's cottage. Grabbing her briefcase, she slammed the car door and hurried towards the police officer who came to meet her.

'Sergeant Black? I'm Dr Grant. I understand you called the surgery?'

'Glad to see you, Doctor.' He shook her hand. The door of the cottage was held open by a woman police officer. 'This is WPC Jones. Any sign of the relatives yet?'

The girl shook her head. 'No, sir, but we're still trying to contact them.'

The sergeant led the way into the cottage. 'I'm afraid it's a nasty business. Has anyone given you any details?'

Jaimie shook her head. 'Only that a patient had

collapsed and has a head wound. I just happened to take the call. I got here as quickly as I could.'

Andy Black's mouth twisted grimly. 'He's through here. A neighbour found him lying on the floor. He was obviously in a pretty bad way so she called us.'

He led the way through a dimly lit hallway into the sitting room, where Ted Hargreaves lay on the floor in front of an ancient sofa. His eyes were closed. A thin trickle of blood was seeping slowly from a wound in his forehead.

At the age of seventy, Ted Hargreaves had worked all his life, making few concessions to the cold of winter or his own advancing years. Even now, with a fire burning in the old lead grate, the small cottage could hardly be described as cosy.

An anxious-looking woman of about forty was standing at the window. She had obviously been crying.

'Mrs Jenkins, this is Dr Grant.'

Edith Jenkins nodded briefly in Jaimie's direction. Her eyes filled with tears and she fumbled in her pocket for a handkerchief. 'It's just awful, and so unfair. Who would do a wicked thing like this? Why, Ted never hurt a soul.' She bit nervously at her lower lip. 'I didn't move him. I found him just like that. I didn't know what to do so I covered him with a blanket and called the police.'

Jaimie nodded reassuringly. 'You did exactly the right thing, Mrs Jenkins.' In one calm, unhurried movement she knelt beside the elderly man to make a gentle examination.

'Mr Hargreaves, can you hear me? It's Dr Grant,' she said gently. 'You've had a bit of a fall. No, don't try to move.'

She reached for her ophthalmoscope, looking briefly into his eyes before uncoiling a stethoscope and applying it to the man's chest. She felt her stomach tighten. His breathing was shallow and uneven. One look at his face told her they were racing against time. If he didn't get help quickly, she didn't think he was going to make it.

Straightening up, she glanced at the sergeant. They moved away from the injured man. 'Where's the ambulance?' she said softly. 'We need it here, *now*.'

'On its way. There was a bad RTA the other side of town. I think they're at full stretch.' He frowned. 'How is he?'

In a lowered voice she said, 'Not good. The head wound isn't as bad as it looks, but he's badly shocked. In someone of his age that's the real worry. There's some bruising on his arms and his pulse is weak. I'm going to give him an injection but I have to be honest—he's not looking too good.'

The sergeant swore softly under his breath. 'I was afraid you might say that.'

He watched as Jaimie filled a hypodermic and administered the injection before she turned to look at him and said quietly, 'What exactly happened here? This wasn't an accident. These injuries weren't caused by a fall.'

He lowered his voice as they moved away again. 'We think there was a break-in. It looks as if the back door was forced open.'

Jaimie stared at him. 'You're saying someone broke in and deliberately did this?'

'It's not the first.' The response was terse. 'We've had a spate of burglaries in the area, but this is the first time they've actually used violence. We think they may have thought the cottage was empty. It's possible the old chap was asleep in his chair. He hadn't switched on the lights and he must have woken up while they were going through his things.'

'And they did *this*?' Jaimie's voice rasped. 'To an old man who couldn't defend himself?' She felt physically sick. 'What kind of monsters are they?'

'The worst kind. Cowards.'

She drew a ragged breath. 'Have you any idea who's responsible?'

Andy Black frowned. 'Knowing it and proving it are two different things. But we'll get them, sooner or later, I can promise you that.'

Jaimie nodded and closed her eyes, blinking hard before turning back to her patient. His pulse was weaker. The bruises already stood out, livid against the pale, paper-thin skin.

She swallowed hard on the lump in her throat. 'Come on, Ted. Hang on, just hang on. Don't give up now. Don't let them win.'

He moaned softly and she held his hand. 'Where is that ambulance? We need to get him to hospital *now*.'

'We've been on to them again. They reckon a couple of minutes.'

'Thank God for that.'

Edith Jenkins began to weep. She was ushered out by the WPC. Jaimie straightened up again and raked a hand through her hair. She sighed, suddenly very weary and very angry. Her head was pounding.

'I'm sorry. I didn't mean to lose my temper. I feel so useless, so angry.' She looked at the man. 'I don't suppose it's easy for you, seeing something like this?'

He nodded and said gruffly, 'Believe me, it doesn't get any easier.'

Minutes later, blue flashing lights announced the arrival of the ambulance. She watched the sergeant stride towards it before she turned and walked out into the early darkness.

She stood in the rain, shivering violently as she watched the paramedics gently lift the stretcher into the ambulance. Then the doors were closed and they were on their way.

Climbing into her car, Jaimie leaned her head back and closed her eyes briefly, feeling sick and exhausted. It was another half-hour before she arrived back at the surgery.

It was empty and in darkness as she let herself in, making her way slowly to her room. Flicking on the light switch, she dropped her briefcase onto a chair. Then, totally illogically, reaction set in and for a brief moment, as tears welled up, she closed her eyes, only to open them again quickly as a voice spoke quietly from the open doorway.

'Are you all right?'

'What?' She blinked hard as Sam walked into the room. 'Oh, yes, I'm fine. You made me jump, that's all. I didn't realise anyone was in.'

She sniffed hard. He frowned as he moved towards her. His hands went around her arms, steadying her as she rocked backwards, and she stared at him a little blankly.

'You're wet through. Are you sure you're all right?'

She swiftly tried to collect her scattered wits.

'Yes. I told you, I'm fine.'

'On the contrary. If you don't get out of those wet

things quickly you're likely to end up with a dose of pneumonia.'

'Rubbish. All I need is a good long soak in a hot bath and some food.' That didn't quite explain why her teeth were suddenly chattering and she wasn't even cold. She fumbled for a handkerchief. 'Anyway, you didn't say what you were doing here.'

'I called in to collect some notes and saw the light was on.' His grasp tightened, turning her to face him when she would have moved away. His gaze narrowed. 'Jaimie, what's wrong?'

A slow tide of colour rose in her cheeks as she looked at him. For some inexplicable reason his touch sent tiny shock waves darting through her. She drew in a deep breath, her face taut with strain.

Blast the man, she thought irritably. It had been a long day. Her head ached and he wanted to know why it had taken her so long to make three simple house calls?

She took a deep breath. Well, maybe she did owe him an explanation at that. She certainly hadn't made too good a job of things, but right now her emotions felt too raw.

'I don't know what you mean.'

His face darkened. 'You're not a very good liar, Jaimie. Something must have happened. You're as taut as a wound spring.' He glanced at his watch. 'I expected you back over an hour ago. You do realise I had to cover evening surgery?'

She stiffened defensively and noticed with a kind of irrationality she could only put down to tiredness that flakes of snow had settled in his hair and that he was wearing an old sweater.

She sighed heavily. 'If you must know, I was called out to see Ted Hargreaves.'

'Hargreaves?' He frowned. 'Hargreaves. Yes, I remember. Elderly chap. He lives a couple of miles or so from here.'

She gave a harsh laugh. 'I'm not sure for how much longer.'

'I don't understand. Jaimie, you're not making sense.'

She said dully, 'I got a call from the police. It seems there had been a burglary. Ted Hargreaves must have surprised the thieves—' She broke off. 'I felt so helpless, so damned useless.' She cleared her throat awkwardly. 'He…he was badly shocked. He'd been hit over the head, or maybe hit it as he fell. Either way, it shouldn't have happened. It shouldn't. It isn't fair.'

'Hey,' he prompted softly, 'you're racing ahead too fast here. I take it you made a proper examination?'

'Yes, of course I did. For all the good it did.' She stared at him, her mouth suddenly dry. 'How could anyone do a thing like that to a defenceless old man? Why?' Tears welled up. 'And what sort of doctor does it make me?' she bit out. 'He was frightened and in pain. An old man, wondering what had happened, what he had done to deserve being treated that way.'

Sam was watching her, a frown drawing his dark brows together. 'You did what you could, what anyone would have done.'

She gave a short laugh. 'And that makes it all right?'

'I didn't say that. I'm simply saying that you're not responsible.'

'Well, someone is.' Her voice broke. 'I saw what

they did to him and I still can't believe any human being could be capable of such mindless violence.' She looked at him. 'It made me think. Maybe you were right. I'm not up to this job. It might be better if I left.'

Suddenly his grip on her arms tightened. 'You don't mean that. You're tired and overreacting, that's all.'

With a sigh of exasperation she started to walk away, and his hands shot out, capturing her arms and pulling her back towards him. His touch had a strange effect on her, sending a tingling awareness of him surging through her, leaving her feeling strangely dazed and breathless.

'I would have thought you'd be pleased,' she said abruptly. 'After all, it's what you wanted. You'll have won.'

The blue eyes returned her gaze steadily, and Sam said softly, 'And what about Jon? Where does he fit into all of this? Or are you so busy thinking about yourself that you've forgotten his needs?'

She gasped. 'That's unfair.'

'Is it?' His mouth twisted.

Her hands were against his chest. She began to struggle and her face flamed as her body made sharp contact with his.

'I'd say we have no choice. We've got to learn to get along together, whether we like it or not. Not just for Jon's sake but for the practice. I'm willing to give it a try. How about you? Can't we at least be friends?'

'Friends!' The word seemed to stick in her throat. Somehow it wasn't a word she felt she could ever apply to her feelings about Sam Paige.

Almost as if he'd read her thoughts, he said softly,

'You really will have to learn not to become emotionally involved, Jaimie. It's a luxury neither of us can afford.'

Was he speaking professionally or personally? she wondered. She stared up at him, bemused. The blue eyes returned her gaze steadily. She saw him tense briefly and was totally unprepared as, very slowly, he bent his head and the sensual mouth moved closer.

It was the sheer unexpectedness of it that caught her off guard. Or, at least, that was what she told herself. Her lips parted on a gasp as he suddenly pulled her towards his powerfully male body, bringing her so close that her nostrils were invaded by the clean, musky smell of him.

For a moment shock widened her eyes as he lowered his head and his mouth took possession of hers with an aggressive thoroughness, forcing her lips apart as his tongue invaded the softness of her mouth.

'Jaimie.' His voice rasped hoarsely as his lips moved over her mouth.

The contact sent a flame of desire rushing through her. It was crazy, she told herself, just as she knew it was quite useless. Sam didn't want her here. He had accepted her presence out of necessity and, besides, he already had a woman in his life—at least one!

Jaimie tensed, willing him to let her go before she made a complete fool of herself. Nothing had prepared her for the almost primordial feeling his kiss had aroused, or her own body's traitorous response.

Sam Paige was, without doubt, the most sexually exciting man she had ever met. A tremor ran through her. She felt both shocked and appalled. What was she doing? She hardly knew this man. It was crazy, but she didn't seem able to prevent it.

Her face lifted to his. She felt him tense, then he set her free, breathing hard.

'It's getting late. You'd better go home and get an early night. We both have a long day ahead of us tomorrow.'

His voice was curt. She couldn't speak. Her pulse was racing crazily. Sam stared at her and his face darkened when she didn't move. 'For God's sake, don't stand there like that.' He turned away and moved towards the door. 'Goodnight, Jaimie,' he rasped. 'Go to bed. I'll see you in the morning.'

She brushed aside a feeling of abject misery. 'I…I can't. I'm on call.'

He swore softly under his breath. 'I'll cover for you.'

'But your date…' She'd suddenly remembered that he had a dinner engagement.

'There'll be plenty of other times,' he said shortly.

She didn't move. 'Thank you.'

'Don't thank me. Just…just go, before I change my mind.' He looked at her steadily then turned abruptly, and a minute later she heard him drive away.

CHAPTER FOUR

WINTER was definitely not over, Jaimie thought as, shivering, she parked her car neatly in the car park at the side of the surgery.

Making her way up the steps and into Reception, she experienced a strange, tight feeling in the pit of her stomach. Having steeled herself to come face to face with Sam, it was something of an anticlimax to find that he had already called in for his notes and had left again.

'Probably as anxious to avoid me as I am him,' she told herself as she shrugged out of her jacket and went to investigate the morning mail.

It was a busy morning, with a steady stream of patients coming and going. The cold weather brought an inevitable rise in cases of bronchitis, as well as an increase in the number of injuries caused by falls.

As one patient left, Paula brought in another batch of cards. 'Sorry.' She smiled wryly. 'These really are the last. Would you like me to bring you a cup of coffee? We're just making some.'

Jaimie was tempted to accept the offer, but she flicked through the pile of cards and shook her head. 'Better not. At this rate we'll still be here at teatime. Who's next?'

'Mr Brady.'

'Right, you'd better send him in, then.'

Jaimie looked up and smiled as Mr Brady entered. 'Take a seat. Tell me what I can do for you.'

Steve Brady smiled weakly as he sat in the chair. Forty, tall and, if anything, slightly underweight, he carefully adjusted the set of his glasses on his nose. 'It's the migraine again, Doctor. If I can just have a prescription for the usual tablets.'

Jaimie brought up his notes on the computer screen. 'I see it's quite some time since you last had an attack.'

He nodded and winced. 'About two years. I thought I'd got over the damned things. It would have to happen now, of all times.'

Jaimie smiled. 'Something special happening, is there?'

'No. Well, not really.' He pulled a face. 'I only started this job about three months ago. I was lucky to get it, especially at my age.'

She laughed. 'Forty is hardly old.'

'It is when there are kids fresh out of university, clutching their degrees and snapping at your heels.' Steve Brady laughed wryly. 'I'd been out of work over a year, and I can tell you I didn't like it. I was lucky to get this job. It was a life-saver, I don't mind telling you. Trouble is, you always have to be on your toes. There's always someone else waiting to step into your shoes if you don't come up to scratch.'

Jaimie nodded sympathetically. 'Yes, I can imagine. And that may be the clue. You said you started the job three months ago.'

'Yes.'

'So you're still learning the ropes, more or less?'

'I suppose you could say that. It's certainly not a nine-to-five job. Well, none of them are any more, are they? And we've just had to switch to new computer software. It meant changing the whole system—up-dating.'

'Well, that's probably your answer. You need to ease up a bit.'

He gave a short laugh. 'I'll tell the boss that when I see him.'

Jaimie looked at him as she handed over the pre-scription. 'I'm sorry I can't do anything about the situation at work, but these tablets should help to get rid of the migraine. They're a fairly new drug. They're fast-acting, which is the main thing, and they should help to ease the queasy tummy, too.'

An hour later the door closed on the last of her patients. Jaimie dictated a couple of letters of referral to consultants at the local hospital and extracted the cassette from the machine, carrying it with the record cards and depositing them on the desk in Reception.

Maggie replaced the phone, put up the 'Surgery closed' sign and nodded in the direction of the nearest consulting room. 'Look, I hate telling tales, but I thought you'd want to know—your uncle is in again.'

'Oh, no!'

'Afraid so. I made some excuse to pop in there about five minutes ago. He said he was just collecting a few things from his desk.'

Jaimie bit back a sigh. 'I'd better go and have a quick word with him before I go out.' She shook her head. 'I don't know what I'm going to do with him. I've tried talking to him but I can't physically keep him away from the surgery.'

Maggie grinned. 'I wouldn't fancy your chances. He's a stubborn man. I think you're fighting a losing battle.'

'So do I. The trouble is, if he doesn't listen to advice I'm afraid he's going to do some real damage. Oh, well, I'll try to talk some sense into him.'

'It's your afternoon off, isn't it?'

'Supposed to be.' Jaimie glanced ruefully at her watch. 'I'd better go and have a chat with him. Oh, by the way, these are a couple of referrals.'

She handed over the cassette. 'If you can get them in the next post I'd be grateful. I want to get Maisie Arkwright's hip operation brought forward if I can. She's hardly able to get about any more. The other is about young Paul Simpson. He needs to see someone about that allergy of his, ideally before he starts school.'

'Leave it with me. I'll see to them.'

Tapping at the door of Jon Reynolds's consulting room, Jaimie popped her head round in response to his command to enter. 'Busy?' she asked pointedly.

'No, almost finished. Come in.' He scooped some papers into his briefcase. 'Just thought I'd catch up on a bit of paperwork at home. You know what it's like. I'm sure the wretched stuff breeds.'

Jaimie studied him dispassionately. His face had a greyish tinge to it and she felt a shiver of anxiety run through her. 'I thought you might like this.' She put a cup of coffee on the desk. 'Uncle Jon, you really shouldn't be here. The doctor said you need to convalesce.'

He rose to his feet, patting her arm. 'Don't fuss, there's a good girl. I never take any notice of what doctors say. I'm as fit as a fiddle.'

'Uncle Jon, you had quite a severe heart attack.'

'Ach! I'm fine. I'm certainly not going to start acting like an invalid now. You know me, can't abide sitting around, doing nothing. The sooner I get back to work the better.'

She joined in with his laughter, but wasn't fooled. He looked tired. Worse than that, he looked exhausted.

Which made it all the more galling when she had to admit to herself that Sam was right. No amount of persuasion, gentle or otherwise, was going to make the older man change the habits of a lifetime. The life of an invalid would certainly hold no charms for a man who had been as active as Jon Reynolds had.

He moved to replace a book on the shelf. 'Anyway, how are you? How are you settling in?'

'Fine.' She smiled. 'I don't think I've had time to feel nervous. I just hope I don't let you down, Uncle Jon.'

'I'm sure there's no danger of that. Don't even think about it. The folk around here are a nice, friendly lot, and Sam's always around if you need any help or advice.'

Perish the thought! Jon obviously set great store by Sam Paige and Jaimie hadn't the heart to disillusion him.

Frustratingly, that didn't make it any easier to put the memory of that kiss out her mind. Telling herself that it had meant nothing didn't help either. After a night of tossing and turning she had simply come to the conclusion that the only way she would be able to stay here and work was if she kept a safe distance between herself and Sam.

'How are you settling into the cottage? I'm afraid it's a bit cramped, but most of our locums are only here for a few weeks, just to cover holidays or emergencies.'

'It has everything I need. Besides, I'm also only here on a temporary basis,' she reminded him, smiling. 'Just until you come back *officially*.'

He chuckled. Jaimie drained her coffee and set the cup down. 'Actually, it's my afternoon off. I thought I might pop into town—look for a few plants, pictures, that sort of thing, just to add a few homely touches.'

'Good idea.' He snapped his fingers. 'Talking of pictures, there a rather nice gallery in town.'

Jaimie grinned. 'I wasn't exactly thinking in terms of real art. More your off-the-shelf-type picture. Just something to brighten up the walls.'

'Oh, I wasn't thinking of anything expensive or too highbrow. No, nothing like that. This gallery specialises in work by local artists. There's some good stuff. I've even bought a few myself.' He foraged in a drawer. 'Ah, here we are.' He handed her a small card. 'The owner is a young chap, easy to talk to, very helpful. Why not go and have a chat with him?'

'Yes, thanks. I'll do that.'

The thought of going into town, of getting away from the practice for a while, seemed suddenly very inviting. If nothing else it would keep her occupied and her mind off other things, she thought with a tiny frown.

With the card tucked safely in her bag, she made her way to the small staffroom, but her hope that she would be able to have a quick cup of coffee and leave before Sam finished surgery were doomed as he came in and accepted a cup from Maggie.

Draining her cup hastily, she rose to her feet and reached for her bag, purposely avoiding his eye. 'Yes, well, if you'll excuse me, I've a couple of calls to make before I do a few errands of my own.' She was halfway to the door when his voice halted her in her tracks.

'If you can spare the time, there are a couple of things I'd like to discuss.'

With a barely concealed sigh she turned and felt herself come under a careful scrutiny which unnerved her as his narrowed gaze seemed to linger on her neatly tailored skirt and the high-necked sweater she was wearing.

'I take it you've recovered from the incident the other day?'

That rather depended on which incident he was referring to! She hastily batted the thought away. 'I'm fine, thanks.'

He nodded and frowned. 'I thought you might like to know, I rang the hospital. It seems Ted Hargreaves recovered consciousness.'

'Oh, thank God.'

'He's still in pain and very frail, not to mention very shocked. They'll be keeping him in for observation for a while. But at least he's improving slowly. Thanks to you.'

She flushed slightly, caught off guard by the unexpected praise. 'Thank you for letting me know. I'd intended phoning the hospital myself later today.'

Jaimie felt her gaze drawn involuntarily to Sam as he stood at the window, but his back was to her, denying her any glimpse of his expression. She wondered vaguely if he knew that the collar of his shirt had seen better days or that his hair needed trimming. She tore her gaze away from it and gave herself a mental shake. 'Well, if that's all…?'

'No.' He turned slowly, making an impatient movement with his hand.

She thought of the visits she still had to do, and the time it would take her to get into town. 'I am in rather a hurry.'

'Really.' His mouth twisted. 'I'm sorry if we're working you too hard.'

'That wasn't what I meant.' She stifled a sigh. 'It's just that I have some calls to make and I also have to go into town on personal business.' She stiffened defensively. 'I'm not asking for any favours. It is my afternoon off.'

He raised one dark eyebrow. 'It's entirely up to you, of course. I was simply thinking that, if it's going to be inconvenient for you, I can always cover the Well Woman clinic this evening.'

Jaimie choked. 'The Well Woman clinic...'

'You hadn't forgotten?'

'No, of course I hadn't.' Not quite true, she thought. She *had* remembered the previous day, but it had somehow completely slipped her mind since then. She swallowed hard. 'Don't worry. I'll be here, and I won't be late.'

She turned on her heel and marched huffily out into Reception before she realised that she still didn't know what it was he had wanted to discuss with her. Dammit! What was it about Sam Paige that he only had to be near her for her usual calm sense of professionalism to fly out of the window?

Ruth was busy filing medical cards on the shelves as Jaimie went up to the desk.

'Oh, Ruth, I'm just off to do a couple of calls. I want to see Mr Taylor. He's still not well after that bout of bronchitis. After that I shall be in Felldale, doing some shopping, but I'll be back in time for this evening's clinic.'

'Fine. I'll see you later. Are you shopping for anything in particular?'

'Just a few ornaments and pictures. Something to brighten up the cottage a bit. It's nice but a bit dull, if you know what I mean.'

'I know exactly what you mean. There's nothing like a few homely touches to make a place feel lived in. There's a gallery...'

'Yes, Uncle Jon gave me the address.' Jaimie smiled wryly. 'I imagine it will be a bit out of my price range, but I'll take a look anyway.'

'I think you might be pleasantly surprised. I've even bought one or two prints there myself. Have a word with Mr Duncan.'

'Duncan?'

'Yes. Giles Duncan. He owns and runs the place. He's a nice man, very easy to get on with.' She glanced sideways at Jaimie, taking in the thick chestnut hair and the fashionable, well-cut skirt and jacket. 'Quite good-looking, too, as a matter of fact.'

Jaimie hunted busily through her bag, searching for her car keys. 'Yes, well, my interests are strictly confined to shopping at the moment. But thanks for the information anyway.' She heard the door open behind her as she hunted for the elusive key, and Ruth looked up.

'Oh, Dr Paige, I was just about to put a call through to your room. Miss Forbes is waiting for you in the car. I explained that you were almost finished here and she said she was quite happy to wait, and to remind you that you owe her a very nice, very large lunch.'

In spite of herself, Jaimie found herself glancing up, and was intrigued by the change that spread across his features, making him seem briefly relaxed. Obviously Miss Forbes had an amazing effect on him, she thought as she reached the door.

It opened before she had a chance to touch the handle, and she almost collided with the figure who came hurrying through.

The girl was probably in her mid-twenties, petite, attractive and with the kind of thick blonde hair Jaimie had always secretly envied. Brown eyes passed with smiling but polite disinterest over Jaimie, then she was laughing and heading straight for Sam's arms.

'Sam, darling, I'm beginning to think you're trying to avoid me. Well, it won't work. You owe me a particularly nice lunch to make up for letting me down last night and, I warn you, I'm ravenous.' She hooked one slender hand through his arm and he was actually laughing as he looked down at her.

'Helen. And there was I, thinking I might get away with a quick pint and a cheese sandwich at the Dog and Duck.'

'No chance.' She grinned. 'I've no intention of letting you off so lightly.'

He bent to kiss her cheek and Jaimie bent to retrieve her bag which had fallen to the floor when she and the girl had met in the doorway.

'Look, just give me two minutes and I'll be with you, I promise.' Sam's look was suddenly directed at Jaimie. 'I'm sure we can safely leave things in Dr Grant's capable hands, for a while at least. Oh, and you won't forget this evening…'

Jaimie scowled. She was in no mood for sarcasm.

Hunched in her jacket, she turned the collar up, gave him a look of disgust and strode out.

She was suddenly aware that her hands were gripping the steering-wheel too tightly and she forced herself to relax. Why should it matter that the woman in Sam's life wasn't just pretty, but, if she were honest, young and strikingly attractive?

It's no concern of mine what he does in his spare time and who he spends it with, she told herself firmly. But all the same a big black cloud, which Jaimie vaguely recognised as depression, seemed to hang over her for the rest of the morning.

As luck would have it, an hour spent poring over a detailed map of the local area last night had paid off, and as a result the calls she had to make didn't take too long.

She had been able to plan a route which led her conveniently back to town, and she was even able to find a parking space, miracle of miracles. Or perhaps it wasn't so much of a miracle since there was a bitingly cold, snow-driven wind and most people with any sense had probably stayed at home.

Locking the car, she headed for the main shopping area and, on impulse, found herself buying a beautifully soft chunky sweater in a shade of deep cherry red she loved.

By the time she came out of the shop it was early afternoon and her stomach was rumbling. She was toying with the idea of finding something to eat and a cup of tea when her eye caught the sign over the art gallery and she decided to delay her hunt for food in favour of looking at the art on display.

She let herself thankfully into the warmth of the gallery. A woman seated at the desk looked up, smiling. A man stood with his back to her, speaking on the telephone.

The voice was pleasant, somehow vaguely familiar, then she dismissed the thought as nonsense, turning her attention instead to the woman at the desk.

'I'm really looking for something to brighten a small room,' she explained. 'Nothing too expensive. I'm not exactly sure how long I shall be in Felldale. I thought perhaps something I could take with me that would fit in anywhere.'

'Did you have anything particular in mind?'

'I'm afraid not. I thought I might just browse and see what caught my eye.'

The woman smiled. 'It's as good a way as any. We've a catalogue if you'd care to look through it. Now where...?' She was busily flicking her way through a filing cabinet when the man put down the phone and turned to speak to her.

His gaze passed briefly over Jaimie with a smile of polite interest and she returned the look. Then her face lit with instant pleasurable recognition while his own changed to one of laughing disbelief.

'You!'

They said it simultaneously and laughed. Jaimie found her hands grasped in a firm handshake.

'Well, this is a fantastic surprise.' His eyes were warm and friendly as he looked at her. 'And to think I'd convinced myself I'd never see my angel of mercy ever again.' He grinned. 'It's not every day a man finds himself wounded and opens his eyes to find a beautiful woman administering to his needs.'

Jaimie laughed. 'Believe me, I don't make a habit of it.'

'In which case I could consider myself doubly

lucky. You'll also be pleased to know that neither do I—make a habit of it, I mean.'

'I'm glad to hear it.' She glanced at the small wound, still evident on his forehead. 'They patched you up, I see?'

His fingers touched the bruising and he winced. 'They did a good job. It needed a couple of stitches, that's all. It looks a bit colourful but it'll be as right as rain in a week or so. I also had concussion, which wasn't very nice, but I was soon over it.'

'What about your arm?'

He flicked back the sleeve of his jacket, revealing a bandage. 'I got off pretty lightly, all in all. This will come off in a couple of days.'

'I was afraid you might have internal injuries.'

He grinned. 'I'm tougher than I look. Lots of bruising, shock.' He looked at her. 'I was very lucky you came along.'

His smile was as attractive as his voice. 'Look, how about a coffee?'

'Well, yes. That would be very nice, if you're sure…?'

He glanced at his watch. 'I was just about to take a break anyway, and it will give us a chance to talk. You can tell me what you're doing here in my gallery, of all places. By the way, we never did manage to get properly acquainted, did we?'

'Not that I recall.' Jaimie chuckled. 'Under the circumstances I suppose it was hardly surprising.'

'Well, I'd say now seems as good a time as any to put that right, wouldn't you? I'm Giles Duncan.'

'Jaimie Grant.'

They shook hands again, laughing. Jenny Palmer, the woman who had greeted Jaimie, sped away, returning minutes later with coffee as Jaimie was explaining her predicament.

'So, you see, I'm really looking for something to lend a little colour. The cottage is very nice. It just lacks those homely touches.'

'I know exactly what you mean.' Smiling, Giles rose to his feet and carried his mug of coffee as he led Jamie slowly round the gallery.

'I'm not looking for anything expensive.'

He laughed. 'Most people aren't. But we still have some excellent paintings.'

'I do think it's a great idea, concentrating on local talent.'

'Why not?' He smiled. 'We're lucky, we have some excellent artists living locally.'

'Oh, I do like those.' Jaimie paused in front of an arrangement of four pictures. 'The colours are wonderful.' She bent her head to look more closely. 'These are local scenes, aren't they?'

Giles nodded. 'The four seasons in Felldale. Painted, believe it or not, by the local vicar.'

He took one of the paintings down from the wall, and for the first time Jaimie realised how tall he was. Good-looking, too, she thought as he handed her the picture.

He was a little older than she had first imagined, probably in his mid-thirties. She flushed as she realised, with a start, that he was returning her gaze.

'Look, I didn't get a chance to say so at the time, but I really am grateful, you know? Things might have been so much worse if you hadn't been around—in the right place at the right time.'

She laughed the comment aside. 'I didn't do much. Dr Paige did most of the work.'

His brows rose. 'You know Sam?'

'Yes. Do you?' Her surprise echoed his own.

'Good Lord, yes. From years back.'

Jaimie frowned. 'I didn't realise he was local.'

'No, I suppose he isn't but, then, neither am I really. I moved to Felldale a few years ago and Sam about two…three. We'd been at the same school. Well, not together exactly. I was several years ahead, but we kept in touch vaguely. You know how it is? You begin with the best of intentions. The gap between letters gets longer. But he came over to Felldale a couple of times and obviously liked the area.'

There was a slight hesitancy to his voice but it was gone so quickly that Jaimie put it down to her imagination.

'Look, are you in a hurry to get back?'

'Well, no, not really.'

He looked at his watch. 'In that case, I've got an idea. You've got a copy of our catalogue and you've had a look at some of the paintings on offer. Why don't we discuss it over lunch? I was going to have some anyway, and afterwards, if there's something you're particularly interested in, we can come back here and deal with the paperwork.'

Jaimie sat down and reached for her bag. 'That sounds nice. I'd love to.' She couldn't help but feel flattered by the look of surprised relief which crossed his face as he grinned.

'Great. I know a pub where they do hot meals as well as snacks, all home-made.'

'It sounds marvellous.'

And it was. Replete after a superb meal, she sat back, drinking her coffee and thinking how easy Giles

Duncan was to get along with. She might have known him for years.

Refusing more coffee, she sat browsing through the catalogue, before folding it and saying decisively, 'It's no good. I'm spoilt for choice. I'm going to go for the four seasons in Felldale.'

'By our local vicar.'

'Absolutely.' She smiled. 'And then when I leave Felldale I'll always have a reminder.'

He frowned briefly and she was vaguely conscious of his arm resting comfortably along the seat behind her.

'Don't talk about leaving, not when we've only just got to know each other.' He smiled. 'Who knows? You may decide you like us too much to leave.' His brown eyes studied her seriously. 'I'm rather hoping you'll want to stay, if you don't mind me saying so.'

Jaimie felt herself blush. 'No, of course I don't mind. It's just that, well, my plans are a little uncertain…'

'Yes, of course. I understand that. Still, we can perhaps do this again some time.' He smiled again. 'I promise, you don't have to buy more paintings.'

Jaimie laughed, breathlessly. 'I'm glad to hear it. I don't think my bank manager would approve.'

'Tell him they're an investment. Seriously, though, if you're sure you want them, I can deliver the paintings for you tomorrow. I'll even give you a hand to hang them if you like.'

It needed only the briefest reflection to decide that she did like. It would be nice to talk to someone outside the practice and about things other than medicine. Apart from that, it took her mind off Sam. 'Yes, I would. I'd be grateful.'

Giles grinned and stuck his hands in his pockets as he rose to his feet. 'I should perhaps mention that I charge very high rates, I'm afraid. At least a cup of coffee and a glass of wine if it runs into overtime.'

'Well, I can't argue with that. It sounds very reasonable.' She laughed and followed him out to his car.

Returning to the gallery, it took just a few minutes to deal with the paperwork.

'There we are, then, all yours. Or at least they will be by tomorrow,' Giles murmured, retaining his hold on the bill of sale for a moment longer than necessary so that his fingers brushed against hers.

Jaimie smiled awkwardly, not unaware that things might be moving rather more quickly where Giles Duncan was concerned than she was ready for.

Or was she complicating things unnecessarily in her own mind? He was a very nice, attractive man, and they were both free agents.

She said briskly, 'Yes, well, until tomorrow, then. I may even have to go out and buy a few tins of paint.'

With the paper tucked into her bag she made her way back to the surgery and, annoyingly, found herself wondering whether Sam had enjoyed his lunch.

CHAPTER FIVE

'I'M SORRY you're not happy in the cottage.'

Jaimie looked up, frowning, from the letter she had just finished signing. The last patient had gone and she had been so busy tidying up a few loose ends that she hadn't even heard Sam come into the room. Now a groove of annoyance edged its way into her forehead.

'What makes you think that?'

'I gather you've decided to introduce a few changes, a few homely touches.'

There was an edge of sarcasm in his voice which she chose to ignore. She flung him a look. 'Nothing too drastic. A few pictures to brighten the walls, a couple of plants. I take it you have no objections?'

He stood with his hands in his pockets, watching her, and she found the experience unnerving. 'Why should I object? The cottage is yours to do as you like with.'

'Good.' Getting to her feet, she found herself deliberately finding things to do rather than sit there being studied. She drew back the curtains from round the examination couch, spending more time than was necessary arranging the folds. 'Actually, it was quite a coincidence. The gallery I went to is run by Giles Duncan, the man who had the accident. You must remember?'

It was her turn to meet his gaze directly now and she felt swift pleasure in the fact that he had the grace to look vaguely discomfited. 'I gather you and he know each other.'

'It was a long time ago. I don't know that that's knowing.'

'Yes, he told me.'

'It's a small world.'

Too small, she thought. 'Giles was very helpful. He gave me some good advice. I bought four pictures by a local artist.'

'Lucky old Giles,' he drawled.

She hadn't been aware that she had used Giles's name until then. It had slipped out quite innocently, but why not? she thought, crossly.

They had lunched together and, under the circumstances, formality would have been ridiculous. Besides, what she did with her private life was nothing to do with Sam, provided it didn't interfere with her work, and there was no chance of that.

She glanced up at him and smiled sweetly. 'Yes, he thought so, too. As a matter of fact, he's coming over this evening after surgery to hang the pictures for me.' She gathered up the case notes, half hoping Sam would take the hint and leave. Infuriatingly, he leaned casually against the desk, watching her with maddening inscrutability.

'You certainly don't waste any time, do you? Are you always so certain about what you want?'

There was something in the way he asked the question that made her head jerk up, her blue eyes uncompromising. 'I try to be. I'm sorry if that doesn't meet with your approval.'

The dark brows narrowed. 'I didn't say I disapproved. What gave you the idea that I would?'

She gave a short laugh. 'Possibly because nothing

I do, or say, seems to meet with your approval.' She slammed the drawer of the filing cabinet. 'Did you want me for something specific, or was this merely a social call?'

To her surprise he gave a low chuckle and she felt an odd fluttering sensation begin in her stomach as he moved round the desk.

'Oh, it was definitely something specific.'

Jaimie felt her colour rise. 'In that case, perhaps you wouldn't mind coming to the point. I'd like to get away on time if possible.'

'Ah, yes, of course, I forgot—Giles is coming over,' he said drily. 'I just wanted to say that I have to attend a conference tomorrow and I'm not sure what time I'll be back. I may be late.' He frowned. 'I suppose I could cancel but I'd really rather not.'

Jaimie frowned. 'I don't see why you should,' she said evenly. 'I can cope perfectly well here for one day. I doubt if the practice is going to grind to a complete halt even in your absence.'

She saw by the sudden tightening of his mouth that she had scored a hit, but for some reason the thought failed to give her the pleasure she had expected.

There was just something about Sam that put her immediately on the defensive, and she didn't like it. It made her feel uneasy.

He looked at her and his mouth twisted. 'I suppose I'll have to take your word for it.' He strode to the door. 'Oh, and, by the way, give my regards to Giles.'

She didn't answer. She was too busy pretending she hadn't heard. Minutes later she heard his car drive away. No doubt the delectable Miss Forbes will soothe his ruffled feathers, she thought, and promptly put him from her mind as she began to gather up her things.

A fire was burning cheerfully in the hearth as Jaimie went to answer the door. Giles followed her into the sitting room, carrying a large, brown paper parcel.

He looked around. 'Mmm, this is very nice. Cosy, neat.'

She smiled as she took his coat. 'I think the word you're searching for is ''small''. Actually, it's not bad.'

'I see what you mean about lacking colour, though. Still, hopefully these will put things right.' He tore the wrapper on the parcel and held up one of the paintings. 'Yes, I think you made the right choice.'

She laughed. 'I seem to recall that I had a certain amount of help. Look, make yourself at home. I'll just go and switch the kettle on.'

'Good idea. If you just tell me where you'd like these hung, I'll oblige.' He set about unwrapping the rest of the paintings, leaving Jaimie to head for the kitchen. When she returned to the sitting room a few minutes later he greeted her with two glasses of wine.

'I hope you don't mind. I brought this with me, just by way of a little thank you and a celebration. I still don't feel I thanked you properly for what you did.'

She felt inordinately touched by the gesture and smiled as she accepted one of the glasses. 'Why should I mind? I think it's a lovely idea, even though it was quite unnecessary.' She sipped appreciatively at the wine. 'Mmm, that's nice. You mentioned a celebration?'

'Just that we met,' he said softly. 'Fate moves in mysterious ways.'

It certainly does, she thought. If she hadn't taken this job, moved into the cottage, walked into the gallery... 'Oh, the pictures.' She glanced at the wall and smiled. 'You were right. They're perfect.'

He made a mocking little bow. 'Our aim is to please and we lay a strong emphasis on the personal touch.'

'You mean you give this kind of service to all your clients?'

'Well, no, only those we like and want to get to know better.' He looked at her. 'I have to admit that I hope this is only the start of a long friendship. You know that, don't you, Jaimie?'

Feeling suddenly awkward, she took a long sip of wine and stared down into the glass. 'Giles, I... Don't let's rush anything. I'd like very much for us to be friends, but let's take it one day at a time. Besides...' she laughed lightly, easing the sudden tension '...there's a grave danger that you might be mistaking gratitude for something else, and I wouldn't want that. Just because I happened to be there at the right time...'

'I don't think there's any danger of me making that kind of mistake.' He leaned towards her and brushed his lips lightly against her cheek.

She made no attempt to prevent it but she got to her feet the moment he released her and he followed suit. Taking the glass from her, he put it on the table.

'I'd better go. You're tired.'

She blinked, suddenly realising that she was grateful to him for understanding and respecting her wariness without referring to it.

'It has been a long day and I have to be up at the crack of dawn.' She looked at him. 'Do you mind awfully?'

'Why should I mind?' With an easy gesture he put his hands on her shoulders and smiled. 'Perhaps I could see you tomorrow? We could go for a meal somewhere.'

'Yes, that would be nice.' Then she grimaced. 'Oh, I can't, not tomorrow. I just remembered, Sam has to be at a conference. He's not sure what time he'll be back so I said I'd cover for him.'

'Oh, well, can't be helped.' He brushed her cheek with his fingers then put her firmly from him with a rueful sigh. 'It's time I went, but I'll call you.'

'Yes, do.' She smiled at him, realising that she actually meant it. It would be pleasant, relaxing, to go out with Giles.

But the idea had already slipped from her mind by the time she had showered and finally slipped between the sheets to dream of Giles. Except that every time she found herself in his arms and looked up into his face, the features somehow, disturbingly, became those of Sam Paige.

CHAPTER SIX

IT HAD stopped snowing and the sun was shining palely, melting the crystal drops hanging from the trees, as Jaimie drove to the surgery the following morning.

It was even possible to convince herself that spring was on the way. Or, if she were more honest with herself, her good mood probably owed more to the fact that Sam was away. Whatever the reason, she wasn't going to spoil it by thinking about him.

She walked into Reception, smiling as she shrugged out of her jacket.

'Morning, Maggie.'

'Hi, you're nice and early.'

'I thought I'd better make a start since I'm going to be holding the fort, so to speak.'

'These are all for you.' Maggie handed Jaimie the mail, which had already been sorted, and Jaimie flicked through it ruefully, recognising the inevitable promotions which detailed the very latest in medical care and new drugs.

'It looks as if I'm in for some pretty dull late night reading,' she said.

'And there's a rep waiting to see you as well.' Maggie smiled sympathetically. She nodded in the direction of the waiting room. 'I did warn him he might be in for a long wait. Do you want to see him now?'

Jaimie frowned. 'How busy are we?'

Maggie consulted the list, sidestepping Paula who

riffled through some papers on the desk, looking for the diary. 'It's not too bad at the moment, but it's still early.'

'In that case, have a word with him. If he just wants to show me some follow-up material on something he's already discussed with Sam, I can spare him…' she glanced at her watch '…five minutes. If it's something that needs more time and my undivided attention, ask him if he wants to wait and see me at the end of surgery or come back before this evening's list.'

'I'll have a word with him now.' Maggie nodded briskly and reached for the telephone as it rang, covering the mouthpiece as she said, 'I was going to ask how you got on at the gallery, but it can wait. Oh, and Dr Paige left this note before he went off to Edinburgh this morning.' She handed Jaimie an envelope.

'He's already been in?'

'So I gather. It must have been early. That was on the desk when I arrived.'

Setting us all a good example, no doubt. Jaimie smiled wryly as she took the letter with her into the consulting room. Well, she for one wasn't impressed. It was probably a long list of instructions, strongly backed with the implication that she wasn't capable of doing her job properly unless supervised. Well, she could do without that, thank you very much.

'You can just sit there and wait until I'm ready for you, Dr Paige,' she said. She propped the letter up on her desk and rang the bell for her first patient.

'Mr Wainwright.' Jaimie smiled, rising to her feet as the man shuffled into the consulting room. 'Oh, dear, can you sit down?'

'It's the back, Doctor.' Jack Wainwright looked at the chair and shook his head. 'If I sit down I might not be able to get up again.'

'In that case, you just stand still and tell me what happened. If you can, loosen your shirt so that I can examine your back. Yes, that's fine.'

'I was digging the garden. Thought I'd try and tidy it up a bit. It's such a mess this time of year.' He grimaced as Jaimie gently probed the painful area. 'Yes, that's it. Right there.'

'I'm sorry if this hurts. I just need to be sure where the pain is actually coming from. Can you lean forward, slowly?' She watched as he attempted it. 'That's fine… No, don't push it. I can see where the problem is. You can tuck your shirt in again now.'

Returning to the desk, Jaimie glanced at her computer notes. 'I see you had the same problem a few months ago.'

'That's right. I saw Dr Paige.'

Jaimie nodded. 'Yes, I see, and what did we give you then?'

'Capsules. Anti-inflammatory or something. I can't remember what they were called.'

'Ah, yes. I've found it. How did you get on with them?'

'Not too bad.' He pulled a face. 'They made me feel a bit queasy after the first few days.'

Jaimie frowned. 'Unfortunately, that can sometimes be one of the side-effects.' She tapped out a prescription. 'Look, we'll try you with something slightly different this time. You take just one a day. They have a time-release action. Hopefully, they'll do the trick, but if not come back and see me again.'

It was a routine surgery, followed by an in-depth

discussion with the sales representative who left her with samples of a new product and a neatly prepared file of yet more informative literature.

It was only as she added it to the growing pile in her briefcase that she remembered Sam's letter. Sighing heavily, she tore open the envelope.

To her surprise it contained not the expected list but a note, written in a large, untidy scrawl.

I thought you'd be pleased to hear that Ted Hargreaves is improving by leaps and bounds. I telephoned the hospital again this morning, before leaving for London. It seems they've also managed to locate a relative—a grandson, who has been living abroad but is now in touch with his grandfather again. He asked that his thanks be passed on to you. Perhaps I can also take this opportunity to add my own thanks for all you did. Events didn't make it seem entirely appropriate at the time!

It was grudging yet, for some inexplicable reason, the words sent a ridiculous surge of pleasure flooding through her. It vanished, however, as she read on.

'I hope to be back in Felldale later this evening, but should you need to contact me urgently, you can reach me at…'

'You should be so lucky,' Jaimie muttered, as her fingers closed angrily over the telephone numbers. 'Well, don't hurry back on my account, Sam. I'm sure you'll be disappointed to hear that we're managing perfectly well without you, thank you very much.'

She grinned as the ball of paper hit the waste-paper bin with a satisfying thud.

It was another half-hour before she finally dropped a bundle of case notes onto the desk in Reception.

'Right, I'm off. Two visits then, hopefully, lunch.' Smiling, she glanced at Paula, then frowned. 'Are you all right?'

'What?' The girl looked up from the paper she was reading. 'Oh, yes, sorry. It's just this piece in the local paper. There's been another burglary.' She shuddered. 'It's frightening enough when you're young, isn't it, to think that a complete stranger can break into your home, go through your most private, personal possessions? I feel so sorry for the elderly. They must feel especially vulnerable.'

Jaimie swallowed hard. 'I know what you mean. I just hope they catch whoever it is before he does any more harm.'

'Is there any more news about Ted Hargreaves?'

Jaimie nodded. 'He's much better, physically anyway. I'm not sure that he'll ever get over the shock.'

It was good to be able to finish the morning calls and go back to the cottage where she had left a casserole in the oven, prepared the night before.

It smelled good and tasted even better, and she found herself eating ravenously as she balanced a tray on her knees and skimmed through the morning paper, before making a start on the list of chores she had promised herself she would do.

On her way back from town she had stopped at the local florist's, and she spent some time arranging to best advantage the flowers she had been tempted to buy.

She stepped back, approving the arrangement, and her eye caught the pictures she had bought from the gallery. Yes, she thought, it was nice to have something of her very own, something she could take with her when she left Felldale.

It was a bit like setting up a home, she thought wryly, except that there was no man around to enjoy her efforts, and somehow when she tried to imagine Giles sitting in one of the large armchairs the picture didn't seem to fit.

But I could make it fit. I just need time to get used to the idea, she thought. In fact, it might be rather nice, coming home in the evening to a warm fireside and a man like Giles. Nice, but not perfect.

Jaimie blinked hard, taken unawares as a fleeting but nonetheless disturbing image of Sam's attractive features flashed, completely unbidden, into her mind, and she wondered what it would be like to be married to such a man.

She shook herself. What on earth was she thinking of, daydreaming about a man she hardly even knew? She rose quickly to her feet. She would have to take Giles up on that offer of a meal some time.

The phone rang and she went to answer it, almost laughing aloud as Giles's voice spoke persuasively in her ear.

'Look, I know this is short notice and I know you're busy tonight, but something's cropped up. I've had an invitation to a dinner party the day after tomorrow and I can take a guest. What do you think?'

'That sounds lovely,' she said with genuine warmth. 'If you're sure?'

'Absolutely.' There was a momentary silence at the other end of the phone, then he said, 'Jaimie, are you all right?'

She could imagine him frowning. She suppressed a giggle. 'Yes, I'm fine. Why?' Perhaps something in her voice had given away the fact that she had been assessing him as possible husband material.

'Oh, nothing. You just sounded a bit…odd, that's all.'

'No, I'm fine. Probably going down with a cold. There's a lot of it about.'

'Well, if you're sure.' His voice sounded husky. Perhaps he was going down with a cold, too. 'I think you need someone to take care of you.' He rang off before she could answer, and she found herself smiling as she made her way upstairs.

It was already quite dark by the time she had a sandwich and a quick cup of coffee, before returning to take evening surgery.

It was late by the time she had finished. Going through to Reception, she signed a couple of letters.

'I'd like these to go in the first post tomorrow.' Jaimie handed them over and glanced, frowning, at the clock. 'Has Sam phoned in yet?'

'Not so far.'

Jaimie frowned. 'It's getting quite late.'

Maggie looked at her watch. 'I'm not altogether surprised. You know what these conferences are like. They do tend to go on a bit.'

'Mmm, I know what you mean.'

'Still, he's lucky you were here to take over. For a while it looked as if he wasn't going to be able to attend after all, what with Dr Reynolds having the heart attack. It would have been a pity. I know this conference was particularly important to him and the organisers had been trying for a long time to persuade him to give the lecture.'

Jaimie frowned. 'You mean Sam is one of the speakers?'

'The *main* speaker. But, then, Sam was probably one of the best authorities on viral meningitis until he decided to give it up.'

Jaimie stared at the other woman. 'I had no idea.'

'Oh, well, I don't suppose he thought it was important for you to know.' Maggie smiled slightly. 'He doesn't talk much about it anyway, not since he decided to give up that side of his work and move to Felldale. I only found out because I typed a couple of letters on the subject for him shortly after he arrived.' She frowned. 'He's a surprisingly shy man, you know.'

Somehow, Jaimie found it hard to believe. She knew she shouldn't encourage the receptionist to gossip, but suddenly she desperately needed to know more about the other side of Sam's character.

'So what made him give it up? Why move to a small, quiet place like Felldale? I mean, it hardly makes sense.'

The telephone rang, breaking the moment for confidences, even had there been any. Maggie reached for it, covering the mouthpiece with her hand. 'I've no idea. As I said, it's not something he talks about and I didn't like to push.'

She reached for the desk diary, flicking open the pages. 'Hello, yes, this is the surgery. Oh, Mrs Clements. No, I'm sorry. Dr Paige isn't on duty this evening. Is it Mr Clements's chest again?' She nodded. 'Yes, I'm sure you are. Look, Dr Grant is here. I can get her to call.'

She glanced at Jaimie who nodded. 'Fine. Doctor will be with you as soon as possible, then, Mrs Clements. No, no trouble at all.'

She replaced the receiver and looked at Jaimie. 'Are you off now?'

Jaimie glanced at her watch and frowned. 'In about five minutes, anyway. I just need to sort out a couple of things for the morning. But you might as well go home if you've finished.'

'Are you sure? Only we're taking my parents out for a meal for their wedding anniversary.'

Jaimie smiled. 'In that case, you must definitely go. Have a good time. I'll see you in the morning.'

Maggie was already on her feet. 'Shall I lock up?'

'No, don't worry. I'll do it on my way out.'

'You won't forget? Only you can't be too careful, what with these awful burglaries.'

'I'll see to it,' Jaimie promised. 'Go and enjoy yourself.'

She went back to her consulting room to collect her bag and a medical journal which contained an article she had been meaning to read for some time.

Except that, somehow, when it came to it and she eventually sat curled up in the armchair in front of a blazing fire, she found herself thinking instead about Sam until, with a sigh of frustration, she realised she was wasting her time.

She wasn't going to be in Felldale long enough to try and unravel the mystery and, anyway, some things, like Pandora's box, were best left untouched.

Even so, lying awake that night and staring up at the shadows on the ceiling, she found her thoughts drifting back yet again to Sam.

It didn't make sense, she decided. Why would anyone give up the satisfaction and prestige that went with such a valuable job to become a GP in a small rural community like Felldale?

Jaimie sighed, tossing restlessly as the more she thought about it the more the answers seemed to evade her.

Peering at the clock, she groaned and fell back against the pillows, flinging her arm across her eyes.

'I can't believe I'm doing this,' she muttered aloud. 'I should be getting some sleep, not lying here worrying about a man I'm not even sure I like.'

She sighed heavily. It was two o'clock. He was probably back by now, safely tucked up in bed and snoring his head off.

For a few seconds the thought presented an intriguing image. She brushed it quickly aside and, with a stifled moan of impatience, flung back the covers, reached for her dressing-gown and padded, shivering, down to the kitchen to make herself a warm milk drink.

It must have helped. Half an hour later she had drifted off into a heavy sleep so that when she woke, suddenly, to the loud trilling of the telephone, she gazed disbelievingly at the clock which now said two forty-five. Shakily she spoke into the receiver.

'Yes. Dr Grant.'

Minutes later she was struggling breathlessly into her clothes as the kettle boiled. She drank scalding black coffee to wake herself up.

Her briefcase was on the table where she had left it. Having flicked a comb through her hair, she grabbed her jacket and ran out to the car, gasping as a wave of cold air hit her.

As she drove it occurred to her that Sam was obviously not back from his conference as her caller had tried his telephone number and had been directed instead to call her.

The road was icy and it needed all of her powers of concentration to keep the car steady. She thought of Sam. He must be exhausted. What if he had had an accident? The thought flashed briefly through her mind and her hand tightened spasmodically on the wheel.

She drew up at the house she'd been called out to ten minutes later. The door opened before she could reach it.

'She's through here, Doctor. The wife's with her.' An anxious-looking man of about thirty led her through into the sitting room where Linda Carter was sitting on the sofa beside her daughter.

The five-year-old was flushed and tearful and seemed to be having difficulty breathing.

'Oh, Doctor, thank goodness you're here. It's Katy. We didn't know what to do. She started coughing and wheezing and she can't seem to get her breath.'

Tim Carter hovered anxiously by the door. 'She's going to be all right, isn't she, Doctor?'

Jaimie made a gentle but thorough examination. She checked the child's pulse and, taking a stethoscope from her briefcase, listened to her chest. It was obvious that the little girl was becoming more distressed and frightened by the breathlessness and barking cough.

Jaimie straightened up, smiled and ruffled the child's hair. 'You're not very happy, are you, sweetheart? And I can't say I blame you.'

She looked at the parents. 'What Katy has is croup.'

'Croup?'

'Yes. It sounds pretty awful and it can be very distressing for the patient.' She looked at Katy. 'But you're going to be all right.' She turned to Linda. 'I'd like you to go up to the bathroom and turn the hot tap on full and close the door.'

The woman stared at her. 'You're not suggesting I give her a bath at this time of the night?'

Jaimie smiled. 'No. Well, not really. What we need is the steam, lots of it. If you can sit in the bathroom with Katy for ten minutes I'm sure you'll see a marked improvement in her breathing. You can pop her back to bed, perhaps use a TV or radio to distract her, or tell her a story. Anything to help her to relax until she goes to sleep again.'

It was almost five o'clock by the time Jaimie finally got back to the cottage to find that the fire had died down. A glance at the clock told her that it was hardly worth going back to bed.

Instead, having tossed a log into the still faintly glowing embers, she made herself a drink, raided the biscuit tin and sat at the kitchen table, wishing that Sam were there.

'I must be more tired than I realised,' she muttered to herself, resting her chin on her hand. The last person she wanted to see was Sam. All the same, his shadowy figure invaded her dreams as, warmed by the cocoa, she drifted into an uneasy doze.

Jaimie woke an hour later, this time feeling even more tired and irritable. She hadn't meant to fall asleep and, having done so, felt worse.

Shivering, she glanced at the clock. 'Please, don't let me have many more nights like this,' she grumbled. 'Come back, Sam. All is forgiven.'

Flinging her clothes off, she took a quick shower then dressed in black jeans and a soft, roll-neck sweater. Staring at her reflection in the mirror, she noted the dark shadows under her eyes and reproved herself for not having had the sense to go back to bed and at least make an effort to get some more sleep. Well, it was too late now.

Rubbing the gritty feeling from her eyes, she decided to take a short, brisk walk. That and several more cups of coffee would just about get her through the day, she thought.

Minutes later, clad in a warm duffle-coat, she was striding out along the lane. Pale sunlight was just beginning to filter through the clouds, and she suddenly realised that in a few weeks the nearby woods would be carpeted in a haze of bluebells.

Jaimie felt a sudden tightening in her chest as she realised that she would probably not be in Felldale to see them.

Returning from her walk half an hour later, she heard the telephone ringing just as she approached the cottage. She fumbled for her keys and ran, breathlessly, to answer it.

'Yes. Dr Grant speaking.'

'At last.' Sam's voice intruded angrily upon her newly restored humour. 'I've been trying for hours to get hold of you. I suppose you've been out wining and dining with dear Giles, and never mind about the patients.'

She couldn't believe he had said it. Her throat tightened at the injustice of the words as she tried to speak.

'As a matter of fact, Doctor—'

'Spare me the details. I'm not interested.' His voice cut in icily. 'I don't have the time. I'm in a call-box.'

'A call-box? But... I don't understand. You were supposed—'

'If you'll give me a chance, I'm trying to explain.

Damn! I'm running out of change.' There was a brief pause, then he continued, 'The conference ran on later than I expected. I tried to get away but couldn't. They'd laid on a meal afterwards. You know how these things are.'

'Well, no, actually—'

'By the time I eventually managed to get away it was snowing hard. I had to stop at one of the motorway services. That's where I am now.' His voice tightened. 'Look, I'm sorry, but I'm not going to make it back in time for this morning's surgery. Can you cover for me? I'll try to get back as quickly as possible. The weather is clearing but it's still going to take a while.'

Jaimie heard her own voice sounding strangely strangled. 'But I've only just—'

His voice cut in sharply again. 'I don't want to know what time you got in, and I don't have time to argue. I'm tired, I need some coffee and a shower. I'm sorry, Doctor, if your work happens to conflict with your social life, but that's not my problem.'

She opened her mouth to fling an angry response at him but the line went dead. He was gone, leaving her shaking with fury.

'How dare he?' she muttered through clenched teeth as she thought longingly of the toast and hot coffee she had been promising herself and rushed instead to spend a few minutes applying a delicate make-up to her face in an attempt to blot out any evidence of her night's 'wining and dining'.

CHAPTER SEVEN

SHIVERING, Jaimie closed the door quickly on a flurry of snow as she made her way through the waiting room into the office.

'Not very nice out there, is it?' Ruth looked up, smiling, as she sorted the morning mail. 'These are for you, Doctor.'

'I know. It's freezing.' Chafing her hands, Jaimie accepted the pile of letters, glancing through them. 'They all look pretty routine.' She frowned. 'I suppose the results of Mrs Watkins's blood tests haven't come through yet?'

'No, sorry. Would you like me to get on to the hospital and see if I can chase them up?'

'Would you? I'd like to be able to put her mind at rest and start her treatment as soon as possible.' Jaimie stifled a yawn. 'Oh, dear. Sorry about that. Do you suppose anyone would notice if I were to go back to bed?'

Ruth grinned. 'They just might. It's pretty full out there, I'm afraid.' She nodded in the direction of the waiting room. 'And I hate to tell you this, but you're on your own. Sam isn't back yet, and I haven't heard from him.'

'No, I know.' Jaimie found it difficult to keep the note of displeasure from her voice. 'He phoned me, from a motorway service area somewhere. It seems he was late getting away from the conference and the weather is delaying him. That's why he called me.'

She knew she hadn't entirely succeeded as curiosity briefly widened the other woman's eyes. 'Still, I suppose it seemed the most sensible thing to do, knowing there would be no one here to man the phones until you arrived.'

She stifled another yawn. 'I just hope there aren't too many problems, that's all. I can't seem to get going this morning.'

'Perhaps you're going down with a dose of this flu that seems to be doing the rounds.'

Now that really would be the final straw. Jaimie shrugged herself out of her coat. 'No. I'm fine. I was called out last night. The Carters' little girl had a nasty attack of croup.'

'Oh, poor little thing.'

Jaimie nodded. 'By the time I got back it was hardly worth going back to bed.' She reached across the desk for a pile of cards and pulled a face. 'All mine? Oh, well, I suppose I'd better make a start. No point putting off the evil hour.'

'By the way, I gather there was another burglary last night.'

Jaimie felt her stomach tighten. 'Have they managed to find out who's responsible?'

'Not yet.'

'Was anyone hurt?'

'Luckily not.'

Jaimie sighed. 'Let's hope they catch him soon. It's all getting too close for comfort. Anyway, I'd better make a start, or at this rate I won't be finished by lunchtime.'

Ruth smiled sympathetically. 'I tell you what, I'll go and make you a nice cup of tea before you start. How about that?'

'You're an angel. And if you could rustle up a couple of aspirins too…'

'I'm sure I can manage that.' Ruth hurried away to the kitchen and a few minutes later put a cup of steaming hot tea and a bottle of tablets on Jaimie's desk. 'Now, you drink that up and I'll send in the first patient in a couple of minutes.'

'What's the betting that every one of them will have complications of one sort of another? I just know it's going to be one of those days.'

It was a relief to find herself proved wrong for once, as the pile of cards diminished at a satisfying rate throughout the next couple of hours.

Jaimie rang the bell for her next patient and a young woman came in with a fractious four-year-old who was obviously running a high temperature.

'I'm sorry to bother you, Doctor,' Mrs Dawson said as she ushered the tearful child into the room. 'Harry's normally such a happy little chap. He's usually rushing around, getting into all sorts of mischief.'

'Don't worry about it.' Jaimie smiled. 'When a child is quiet it's usually a pretty good sign that something is wrong. So, Harry…' She smiled and made a swift, professional assessment of the flushed child. 'I hear you're not feeling too well?' She moved her chair to sit beside him, taking one small hand in her own. 'Shall we see if we can make you feel better?'

In fact, it scarcely needed an examination to tell Jaimie what she already suspected, that it was a textbook case of chickenpox, but she made the usual investigations, before straightening up.

'Well, I'm afraid it's chickenpox. The spots are just beginning to appear, which means that by tomorrow morning he'll probably have lots more.'

The woman sighed. 'He's not going to be happy, is he?'

Jaimie grinned. 'Probably not.'

'I should have known. Half the kids at playgroup have been going down with it for the past ten days or so. I was hoping we might be lucky and get away with it.'

'If it's any consolation, it's better he has it now than when he's older. In a few rare cases chickenpox in adults can cause some quite dangerous complications.'

Getting to her feet, she followed Annie Dawson to the door.

'I don't suppose he'll have much of an appetite for the next few days, but try and get him to drink plenty of fluids. A dose of Calpol will help to bring his temperature down.' She ruffled the child's hair. 'I'm sure he'll be as right as rain in a few days.'

Jaimie had just seen the last patient out and was tidying her desk when someone tapped at the door and came in. She frowned and did a hasty recount of her cards because she was certain Paula had said there were no more patients. Her frown deepened as she saw Sam.

Her heart missed a beat. He was carrying his jacket slung over his shoulder. Faded jeans hugged his lean hips and thighs, emphasising his maleness. Beneath his black sweatshirt his powerful shoulder muscles moved in taut definition.

Jaimie rose to her feet, glancing witheringly in his direction. His comments earlier still rankled and she said stiffly, 'I'm afraid you're too late. Surgery is over and I'm sure you'll be pleased to hear that I've managed not to lose or upset a single patient. I assume that's why you're here. To check up on me.'

Immediately she wished the words unsaid as he dragged a hand wearily across his forehead. 'No, as a matter of fact, that isn't why I'm here. If I'd had any doubts about your competence, believe me, I wouldn't have let you loose amongst my patients.'

She flashed him a look. 'I see. So maybe it was simply my morals that were in doubt.'

'Oh, that.' He studied her, taking in the firm set of her mouth, the truculent angle of her jaw. His brows drew together in a frown. 'I've upset you.'

'Upset!' Her head jerked up and she gave a short laugh. 'Yes, I think you can safely say I'm upset. Contrary to what you may think—'

'Look, I didn't come here to argue with you. I'm bloody tired and I'm not exactly in the best of tempers.'

'So what's new?' she snapped uncharitably.

'For crying out loud, you could try to make this easier.'

She sent him a withering look. 'You should be so lucky.'

Sam stared at her and drew a deep breath. 'I was actually worried sick about getting back here, about leaving you to cope alone. Not,' he added quickly, 'for the reason you obviously think. The truth is, I scarcely remember what I said.'

He ran a hand through his hair, leaving a tuft standing on end. It made him look younger, oddly vulnerable, and for one crazy moment Jaimie had to stifle an impulse to go to him and smooth it down. She drew herself up sharply.

'How very convenient. Unfortunately, I remember

every word, and I have to tell you, Dr Paige, that I resent being spoken to in such a manner.'

'Even though it was justified?'

She stiffened. 'It may come as something of a surprise to you, but off duty I am free to do as I please, see whom I please. I don't need your permission. What I choose to do in my private life is nothing whatsoever to do with you.'

A glimmer of something suspiciously like amusement flickered in his eyes. 'I agree. Provided it doesn't affect your work.'

Colour flared defensively in her cheeks. 'That's unfair. I've never done anything that would interfere in any way with my work and you have no right to suggest otherwise.'

There was a short silence then his dark brows drew together. 'You're right. What you do with your life is none of my business. As for what I said:...I can only say I'm sorry. I spoke in the heat of the moment. I know that my comments were completely unjustified and the fact that I was tired was no excuse.'

Jaimie stared at him, open-mouthed. 'You do? I mean, you know? But—'

'I've spoken to Ruth.' His mouth twisted into a wry grin, before sobering again. 'She told me how things have been—that you were called out and didn't get back till the early hours.'

'As I would have told you had you given me the chance.' At least he had the grace to look sheepish, she thought.

'I realise that now. But I was worried. Conferences are not my favourite things, especially when I'm the speaker. And, contrary to what you may think, I did feel guilty about asking you to shoulder the burden here. You have rather been thrown in at the deep end since you arrived.'

Incredibly, she found her defences crumbling. She smiled slightly. 'I rather thought that was the idea, that I should relieve you of some of the burden.'

'Jon's idea, not mine.'

She gave a sigh of exasperation. 'Must you always be so pig-headed?' Her gaze flew up to meet his and found his eyes regarding her with mocking amusement.

'Look, I've got an idea. Why don't we call a truce? You're right,' he said softly. 'I've not been the best of people to work with, but these past few months haven't exactly been easy on any of us.'

She offered him a reluctant grin of her own. 'Well, I can understand that. I'm concerned about Jon, too, you know. He means a lot to me, but it isn't going to help if we're constantly bickering, is it?'

Sam sat on the edge of the desk, watching as she tidied it without really thinking about what she was doing. She turned her head and looked into the tense features and a tremor of something closely akin to excitement ran through her.

It was happening again. His nearness was making her uneasy. Suddenly his hand came down over hers, halting its movements, and her breath snagged in her throat.

'Truce?' he murmured softly. 'Is it too much to ask?'

She gazed at the sensual mouth and swallowed hard. 'No, I suppose not.'

'We could start by you calling me Sam. It is my name, you know.'

He straightened up slowly and her lips parted on a

gasp as he slowly drew her towards him, bringing her so close that she was aware of the clean, musky smell of him.

Her breath caught in her throat and she said huskily, 'Well, I suppose it's worth a try, Sam.'

For a second she stared at him, shock briefly widening her eyes as his gaze narrowed. She heard his soft intake of breath and she stood, mesmerised, as slowly he bent his head and kissed her.

His mouth brushed lightly, teasingly almost, against her lips at first, and then, as she drew a quivering breath, the pressure deepened until his kiss became more demanding and, moaning softly, she swayed towards him.

She was stunned by the power of the sensations that coursed through her. Her head went back as his fingers sought and found the fullness of her breast. His breath fanned her throat as he stared down at her.

It was utterly crazy, she told herself as his grip tightened, sending a tingling awareness surging through her. Truce, he had said, not total surrender. If this was war, someone should have told her the rules of engagement. She wasn't ready for this.

She had been kissed before but never like this, and she heard her own swift gasp of shock as the contact renewed all the previous fire of that other encounter.

The phone rang. She gasped disbelievingly.

'Ignore it,' he rasped. His lips drew her own back, but with the strident ringing common sense returned rapidly and she pushed him gently away, trying to steady her breathing.

'I can't. It might be urgent.'

'This is urgent.'

She groped behind her for the phone, fumbling for

the receiver as Sam's face followed her own until she deliberately tilted her head out of his reach and said breathlessly, 'Yes? Dr Grant speaking. No, of course you're not disturbing me.'

Sam nibbled wickedly at her ear. 'Tell whoever it is that I'm taking care of that, thank you very much.'

He wasn't making this easy. In desperation she pushed him away as the voice said, 'Hello. Hell! This must be a bad line. Jaimie? I hope I haven't called at a bad moment.'

She stifled a groan. 'No. Not at all.'

'Only I thought surgery would be over.'

'Yes, it is.' The laughter slid from her eyes, taking with it some of the giddy sense of elation. 'G-Giles. Hello, no, it's fine. Surgery finished a while ago. I was just…clearing up.'

'Oh, good. It's lucky I caught you, then.'

She was vaguely aware of Sam straightening up, his face suddenly expressionless. She wanted to draw him back, to regain the moment.

Her voice shook. 'Yes, it is.' Her eyes followed Sam to the door, silently pleading with him to wait, but Giles's voice held her relentlessly. 'I just thought I'd better call to remind you about tonight. Shall I pick you up about eight?'

'Tonight.' Of course, he was taking her to dinner. Her brain worked feverishly and her spirits sank. 'Oh, yes, that will be fine.' What she wanted to say was, I've changed my mind. I need my own time right now.

She dropped the receiver into place and turned to see Sam standing at the door, his face suddenly like that of a stranger again. The kiss might never have been, except that her lips still felt swollen from the pressure of his mouth.

'I'd better get going,' he said evenly. 'Obviously you're needed elsewhere.'

'Sam…' Her voice dragged out his name but she knew it would be pointless to go after him. 'Look, it isn't what you think. I arranged a couple of days ago to go out to dinner with Giles tonight.' She didn't know why she offered the explanation. The words seemed garbled even to her own ears.

'It's all right. I understand perfectly. And you're right. What you do outside this practice is none of my business.'

His voice sounded so unfamiliar, so cool, that she almost flinched.

The door closed and she was shocked to find her eyes filling with tears. 'Damn!' she swore under breath. 'Damn! Damn! Damn!'

Then she mentally shook herself. After all, wasn't she reading too much into one simple kiss which, judging from Sam's expression as he'd walked out of the door, obviously hadn't meant anything to him?

Except that it hadn't been a simple kiss, she thought. Because surely no simple kiss left you feeling as if your entire body were on fire.

CHAPTER EIGHT

SEATED at the kitchen table, Jaimie ran her gaze briefly over the day's mail, her mind half on the slice of toast that was her lunch.

Spotting an item of local interest, she read intently, warmed by the shaft of late afternoon sunshine which streamed in through the window, highlighting the chestnut tints of her hair. The sun emphasised the generous contours of her mouth which presently bore a slightly downward curve.

Abandoning the toast, she poured herself another cup of tea and toyed briefly with the idea of phoning Giles and cancelling their date, pleading that she felt unwell.

She did have a headache. Hardly surprising under the circumstances, she thought, stifling a yawn. But on reflection it seemed cowardly to use something which she knew was purely mental rather than physical as an excuse.

Swallowing a couple of aspirins, she rested her chin on her hand and briefly closed her eyes. It was ludicrous to find herself actually resenting a whole afternoon of unplanned idleness.

It was a luxury she had been promising herself since her arrival in Felldale, but now that the opportunity had presented itself somehow the prospect of spending the time on household chores had definitely lost its charm.

Yawning again, she came to the conclusion that an

evening with Giles might be quite enjoyable. At least it would be uncomplicated, she decided and, having eaten the last of her toast, went up to the bedroom to scan the contents of her wardrobe and decide what she would wear.

Five minutes later she was beginning to panic. When she had come to Felldale it had been with the sole notion that she had been coming to work. A social life hadn't been part of her plans, and now that she looked at the one dressy outfit she had brought with her it seemed not only dated but dull.

'I'm out of touch,' she said to her reflection. 'What I need is a make-over. But am I likely to find it in Felldale, I ask myself?'

Ten minutes later, all thoughts of chores abandoned, she was in the car, heading not for Felldale but for the nearest large town, several miles away, where she managed to get her hair shampooed and styled.

She emerged from the salon with her chestnut curls flicked into a new gamine style which boosted her morale and turned the hunt for a new outfit into a necessity rather than a chore.

Without knowing exactly what she was looking for, she found it, gasped a little at the price, but came out of the boutique clutching a bag which contained a beautifully cut, short, slim-fitting black dress and matching jacket.

Her purchase made, she drove to see Jon. She had promised her father that she would keep an eye on him and report on his progress, just to put his mind at rest.

She arrived at the house, however, to be met at the

door by Mrs Barnes, the housekeeper, whose worried face cleared with relief as she saw Jaimie.

'Oh, Dr Grant, thank goodness it's you. Perhaps you can talk some sense into him because I can't. I've done my best but he just won't listen. Stubborn as a mule he is, and I've told him so. Not that it makes any difference.' Alice Barnes shook her head unhappily. 'All I get for my pains is to be told that I'm an old fusspot. Fusspot, indeed. I've never heard the like in all the years I've worked for him.'

Jaimie felt her spirits sink. 'Why, whatever is he up to?' She hurried in, depositing her jacket and gloves on the hall table. 'I'm sure he doesn't mean to snap at you, Mrs Barnes. It's not like him.'

'No, I know that. Which is why I'm so worried. I know he's not himself when he gets like this, but you'd think a man his age would listen to sense. I've seen two-year-olds better behaved and that's the truth.'

Trying to hide a feeling of alarm, Jaimie smiled. 'In my experience doctors always make notoriously bad patients.'

'That's the trouble. He won't accept that he is a patient, or that he needs to take care. I thought I'd surprise him with a nice tray of tea and biscuits in his study and walked in just in time to catch him moving the furniture around.'

'Oh, no!'

'Oh, yes. Shifting the desk he was. Books and papers piled everywhere, and he's moving it across to the other side of the room. Wants it nearer the window, he said. As if it couldn't wait until he had some help.'

Mrs Barnes flapped her hands as if flapping the

vision away. 'His face was as white as a sheet and he was puffing. Well, I said my say and he didn't like it, so perhaps you can talk some sense into him because I don't intend getting my head bitten off for my pains. I'll go and make some more tea. I think I've earned a cup.'

She stormed off in the direction of the kitchen, leaving Jaimie to make her way into the study with a lecture already on her lips. It faded abruptly as she saw Jon sitting in the chair. He looked pale and his eyes were closed. He was breathing deeply.

Jaimie felt her heart miss a beat as she went quietly towards him but his eyelids flickered open as she stood there uncertainly.

For a moment he seemed confused as he looked at her, then he blinked in recognition and said crossly, 'I hope you haven't come to give me a lecture, too, because if you have you can go away again. I've already heard it from Mrs Barnes and I told her she's an interfering old woman.'

He broke off and leaned forward to press a hand to his chest. Jaimie tried to keep from her expression the sudden and very real concern she felt as she moved to sit in the chair opposite.

'Well, that wasn't very kind, was it?' she said smoothly. 'And what makes you think I'm here to lecture you? Unless, of course, you've been doing something you know you shouldn't?' She looked pointedly at the piles of books and papers and the desk standing in the middle of the room.

'I don't need to be told what I can and cannot do in my own home. Damn lot of fuss about nothing.'

'Don't you think you're being just a little unfair to Mrs Barnes?' Jaimie prompted gently. 'She worries about you, you know. Besides, she's right, you aren't supposed to be overexerting yourself.'

'I've absolutely no intention of sitting around in a chair, doing nothing all day. A little exercise is good for me.'

Jaimie gave a short laugh. 'But we're not talking a little exercise here, are we, Uncle Jon? I'm sure the doctor didn't quite have in mind that you should start moving furniture. Couldn't it have waited?' She eyed him firmly and he had the grace to look sheepish.

'This sounds very much like a lecture to me.'

'Well, I'd say you deserve it. As a matter of fact, I came to see how you are. Dad was asking.'

'Huh. And I suppose he said you should keep an eye on me?'

'He knew I'd do that anyway.'

'Well, you can tell him I'm fine, just fine.'

Jaimie met his gaze directly. 'I'm not sure I can do that. Unless you promise me you'll stop moving furniture and behave sensibly from now on.' She frowned. 'You don't have to prove anything, Uncle Jon, and there's no shame in admitting that for once in your life you have to take things easy. What were you trying to do anyway?'

'What does it look like?'

'Frankly, I'm not sure.'

'I've been meaning to shift that desk for years. It'll get the full light from that window over there, and I can look out onto the garden.'

Jaimie looked up with relief as Mrs Barnes came in with a fresh tray of tea and a look passed between the two of them.

'And you needn't think I don't know what's going on.' He helped himself to the only chocolate biscuit on the plate. 'You needn't think I don't know the pair of you are ganging up on me.'

'I don't know what you mean, Uncle Jon. We just don't like to see you taking unnecessary risks, that's all. Besides, if you asked him I'm sure Sam would be only too pleased to move the desk for you.'

'I dare say he would, but he's got more than enough on his plate as it is. How are you two getting on, by the way?'

Jaimie stirred sugar briskly into her tea. 'Fine. No problems at all.'

'Yes. That's what he said.'

She choked on a crumb and spent the next few minutes coughing, but at least it diverted her thoughts to other things.

Before she left she and Mrs Barnes moved the desk into the window bay and spent the next half-hour gathering up piles of books and files and setting up the word processor.

She was just glancing at her watch and thinking it was time she left when Sam walked into the room. He didn't seem particularly surprised to see her, but he had probably seen her car parked in the drive anyway.

'Sam.' Jon held out his hand. 'It's good to see you. This must be my day for having visitors. Jaimie decided to check up on me as well. You could have come together.'

'Yes, I suppose we could. A pity we didn't think of it.' Sam's dark head moved in brief acknowledgement before his glittering gaze moved with slow deliberation to Jaimie.

A tremor of desire ran through her as his eyes travelled over her. Her body responded as though he had touched her, sending a wave of heat rushing through her.

He bent forward to examine the teapot and poured himself a cup, before proffering the pot in her direction. She shook her head.

'No, thanks. I've already stayed longer than I'd intended.' She glanced at her watch again. 'Oh, lor, is that the time? I must get back.'

'Ah, yes.' He leaned nonchalantly against the desk. 'I was forgetting—you have a date. Well, I'm sure you won't want to keep Giles waiting.'

Colour flared defensively in her cheeks as she brushed a hand across her face, conscious of the dust which had settled on her from the books.

'No, you're right, I won't.' She kissed Jon and walked to the door where she turned to smile at Sam. 'By the way, do be sure to give my regards to Miss Forbes.'

She didn't wait to see what effect her parting shot had. The growl in his throat was sufficient to send her almost running out to the car, then she laughed involuntarily as she started the engine, and said aloud, 'One to me, I think, Dr Paige.' Though for some reason there was surprisingly little satisfaction to be found in the thought.

Back at the cottage, Jaimie took herself to the bathroom to indulge in a leisurely soak in her favourite foaming bath oil. Her hair needed nothing more than a quick brushing until the chestnut waves shone. Her make-up she applied slightly more heavily than she would have worn during the day.

The effect when finally she stepped into the black dress was both dramatic and stunning. She was applying touches of her favourite perfume when, right on cue, the doorbell rang.

She slipped her feet into slender-heeled shoes and went to answer it, purposely pausing to check the contents of her evening bag on the way.

Giles greeted her with a kiss and a bunch of roses as he gazed with undisguised admiration as she performed a twirl for his benefit.

'I didn't know what to wear so I went out and bought this.' She came to a halt, frowning anxiously. 'You don't think it's too short, do you?'

'Certainly not. I think it's absolutely perfect.' Taking her in his arms, Giles kissed her and she returned the gesture passively.

She wasn't going to allow her evening to be ruined by Sam Paige. All the same, she couldn't help wondering how he would have reacted had she gone to so much trouble for his benefit instead of Giles's. An uncomfortable awareness came to her that, in a way, it almost *had* been for his benefit—a kind of defiant gesture and a totally pointless one at that, she reminded herself crossly, because he wouldn't be there to see it.

She was unaware that she'd sighed involuntarily until Giles put his arms round her and studied her with a look of concern. 'You do want to go tonight, don't you? I did rather push you into it.'

She smiled, cross with herself for having let her thoughts show. 'Yes, of course I want to go. I'm looking forward to it.' Not as much as if it had been Sam standing there. The thought rose provocatively to tease her and she pushed it away. 'I'm just a little out of practice at socialising, that's all.'

'Oh, is that all? Well, I promise you, you don't

need to worry. It's not exactly a crowd. Just Alan Latimer—he has a small antiques business in Felldale—and his wife, Sonia. It's their party and I know you'll like them. And there's Bill Watkins and his wife. Bill's the local vet, well, one of them anyway. Works for a partnership in town, and Laura is some kind of financial advisor.'

'Lucky Bill, having someone to look after the books.' Jaimie smiled. 'Talking of books...' She groaned and went on to relate sparingly the details of her afternoon while he finished his glass of sherry and she hunted for her handkerchief.

It was a relief to discover that the Latimers were indeed nice, ordinary people who went out of their way to make her feel at home.

Sonia Latimer was a slim, petite woman of about forty, her dark-haired good looks dramatically emphasised by the deceptively simple, figure-hugging dress she was wearing.

She led Jaimie upstairs to fresh up 'while the men pour out some drinks and get the shop talk out of their systems'. She sat on the bed while Jaimie flicked a comb through her hair and checked her make-up.

'I'm so glad you could come,' she said. 'We've heard so much about you from Giles. He says you're a doctor and I know they are notoriously busy people.'

'I imagine the antiques business must have its moments, too. I gather you have a shop in Felldale?'

'Yes. We bought the business about ten years ago. I suppose it was a bit of a risk but I have to say it's doing rather well,' she boasted with a pride which lit up her attractive face.

'Is that how you came to know Giles, through the business?'

'Oh, yes. He runs a gallery, you know. Well, yes, of course you would. He and Alan met at a few of the sales and got to know each other and Alan lets Giles know if something he thinks Giles might be interested in comes into the shop.'

Jaimie laughed. 'Sounds like a good arrangement to me. Not,' she said wryly, 'that I know the first thing about art or antiques.

'Neither did I to begin with. But you learn as you go along and that's what counts. Anyway, come on. Let's go and see whether they've got around to discussing European currency yet.'

They went downstairs just as the doorbell rang and Bill Watkins arrived with his wife. She was a pretty girl to whom Jaimie took an instant liking.

'Alan tells me you're acting as locum for Dr Reynolds until he gets over his heart attack.'

'Yes, that's right.'

'You're not thinking of settling permanently in Felldale, then?'

Jaimie smiled. 'It's a tempting thought, but I don't imagine I'll be here for more than a couple of months.'

She wondered whether she had imagined the quick glance that passed between Alan and Sonia.

'Dr Reynolds's illness was a tremendous shock to people around here. Most of them have known him all their lives. He *is* getting better?'

Jaimie sipped at her drink, trying unsuccessfully to banish from her mind the picture of him as he had been that afternoon. 'He does seem to be improving. He'll need to take things easy for a while, of course.'

'And you'll be staying in Felldale until he's well enough to join the practice again? I know Giles will be pleased about that.'

Jaimie fudged an answer, partly because she didn't want to become involved in a professional discussion and partly because she saw Giles glance in her direction with the kind of look that seemed to be asking the sort of questions she was far from being ready to answer.

She smiled at him over her glass. He looked nice in a grey suit, and the lights picked out a few strands of grey hair so that for the first time she became conscious of the age difference between them.

Not that something like that mattered these days. There was even something quite reassuring in the way his hand came to rest proprietorially on her arm.

He smiled as they followed the others into the dining room and said quietly, 'I'm sorry, I promised myself we wouldn't talk shop. But I'm afraid I've made no secret of the fact that I'd very much like you to stay in Felldale.'

He hesitated and they were left alone to chat against a background of music coming from a subdued stereo.

'I hope you don't mind, Jaimie. I hadn't intended saying anything, not so soon. If the discussion hadn't got around to you leaving…' He frowned. 'I suppose it suddenly brought home to me the fact that I could lose you.'

'No, of course I don't mind.' But for some reason embarrassment gave a faint edge to her voice and she looked up, suddenly serious. 'Giles, I'm flattered that you feel the way you do but, please, don't…don't get too serious. Not yet. It's all happened so quickly. I'm not ready…'

'I know.' His hands rested on her shoulders. 'It's taken me by surprise, too. I really didn't mean for this to happen, but the truth is that I've become very fond of you, Jaimie. If I'm honest, more than fond.'

He looked at her and his finger gently brushed against her cheek. 'I'd just like to think there might be a chance that I could persuade you to stay and that, in time, we might be more than just friends.'

Jaimie found herself battling with a tiny sense of panic. Things were getting out of hand. She was being dragged into something deeper than she was prepared to go at this stage. 'Giles, I—'

He silenced her with a kiss. 'It's all right,' he said softly. 'I understand. It's too soon and you're not to worry about it. I'm not asking you to marry me.' He laughed. 'Not quite yet anyway.'

With an effort she summoned a smile. Her mouth felt dry.

'Are you two coming? We're all waiting to eat in here.' Sonia smiled at them from the doorway.

'Just coming.' Almost too quickly, Jaimie moved towards the dining room to take her place at the table. She was very fond of Giles. She enjoyed his company. He had the sort of qualities she liked in a man. But were they the kind of qualities which made for marriage?

She was relieved when, several hours later, they arrived back at the cottage and Giles made no suggestion that he should come in. Instead he kissed her gently.

'I've really enjoyed myself this evening. It's been

lovely but I won't invite myself in for a nightcap. We both have a busy day ahead of us tomorrow.'

He kissed her again and Jaimie was aware of a vague stirring of her emotions. But they were nothing like the sort of emotions she had experienced when Sam had kissed her.

Did that matter? she wondered while she lay in bed some time later. She sat up, plumping her pillow crossly with her fist, and closed her eyes firmly. But not firmly enough to blot the image of Sam Paige out of her thoughts completely.

CHAPTER NINE

JAIMIE woke next morning with a splitting headache, the result of too much coffee, too much excellent food and too little sleep.

And to make matters worse, she opened her eyes to the horrifying realisation that she had also overslept. Maybe because she'd had her mind on other things or simply because she'd been overtired, whatever the reason, she'd forgotten to set the alarm, with the result that she arrived at the surgery breathless and cross.

'Morning, Maggie. Hi, Paula. Sorry I'm late. I'll just collect my things. Give me a couple of minutes to get myself organised then you can send in the first patient."

Hurrying through Reception, Jaimie paused briefly to gather up a pile of patients' cards, but any hopes she might have had of being able to get in quietly and unnoticed were dashed as Sam appeared just as she was heading along the corridor towards her room.

For an instant their eyes met and she knew he was angry. The fact that his anger was justified made it, if anything, worse, and she pushed open the door, scuttling into her room, glad that he was busy seeing out a patient at that moment, thus giving her at least a temporary respite. Somehow she managed to get through the morning's list. She saw the usual crop of sore throats and a number of patients who seemed to be suffering from flu and all its varying symptoms.

Why they didn't simply take to their beds and dose themselves with whatever kind of remedy suited them best, rather than coming to the surgery, was a mystery she felt too tired even to fathom.

Her own headache had worsened to the point when, having seen the last of her patients, she went gratefully in search of coffee, took her own advice and was just hunting in her bag for some painkillers when Sam walked in.

He poured himself a cup of coffee and frowned as he spooned in a generous helping of sugar.

She smiled wryly. 'Great minds think alike.' She proffered the bottle of aspirin. 'These may help.'

His dark brows edged together. 'Somehow I doubt that.'

Perhaps he'd had a bad night, too, she told herself resignedly. Looking at him, she experienced a brief sense of shock. He looked tired. More than tired, exhausted. That, she told herself, might account in part at least for the note of irritability in his voice. But she certainly wasn't prepared for the vehemence of the attack he launched on her.

'I suppose I should at least be grateful that you managed to get here at all. I hope you don't intend making a habit of bringing your hangovers to the surgery. It doesn't exactly provide the sort of image we want to present to our patients, any more than arriving late does.'

As she stared at him, open-mouthed, his cup rattled into the saucer and he put it down on the table. 'Frankly, if you can't keep your social life and your working commitments apart, then you're not doing your job properly and you're not a lot of use to me.'

Her eyes flared with shock and resentment. How

dared he? His brooding glance slanted over her, no doubt taking in the shadows beneath her eyes and drawing his own conclusions as to their cause. But if he thought she was going to meekly accept being judged without saying a word in her own defence, he had another think coming.

'That is grossly unfair.'

'Is it?' He brushed the back of his hand against his forehead. 'Unfortunately, I've neither the time nor the inclination to argue the point. I've got calls to make. I imagine you have, too. In any case, I'm really not interested in listening to excuses.'

'Well, bully for you because I don't intend making any.' She faced him, breathing hard, saw the momentary narrowing of his eyes and ignored it. 'You can have an apology. I forgot to set my alarm and I overslept. I admit it was stupid of me, but it won't happen again.'

'Perhaps I should be grateful for small mercies.'

Jaimie had to resist a strong urge to slap his face, then found herself wondering if the thought had actually precipitated the action as he pressed a hand to his head and briefly closed his eyes.

Concern momentarily overcame other instincts as she moved towards him. 'Are…are you all right? You look awful.' It was true. His face was ashen.

'Yes, I'm fine,' he said peevishly. He straightened up. 'It's just this damned headache.'

'A hangover, is it?' she suggested caustically, and, shaking a couple of aspirins into her hand, slapped them firmly into his. 'I can recommend these. They do wonders for sore heads. I suggest you take several, and now, if you'll excuse me, Doctor, I have work to do.'

She turned briskly on her heel, vaguely aware that he swore softly under his breath.

'Jaimie, wait!'

She resolutely ignored him. So much for a truce, she thought as she walked into her consulting room and firmly closed the door behind her. Next time she wouldn't waste her sympathy. Except that there wouldn't be a next time, would there? It was a thought that did nothing to lift the cloud of depression which suddenly seemed to be sitting just above her head.

Ten minutes later she heard Sam drive away. It was half-day closing at the surgery. The waiting room was empty. It was Ruth's day off and Paula had gone to the dentist.

Jaimie deliberately lingered at her desk, glad of the peace and quiet as she finished off a couple of letters, signing them with a flourish.

Maggie tapped at the door and popped her head round. 'I'm just off. I'll post those on my way home if you like.'

'Oh, would you? You're an angel.' Sealing the envelopes, Jaimie handed them over.

'Will you be long?'

'No, I'm just about finished.' Jaimie stretched her arms and eased her aching shoulders.

'Shall I lock up on my way out?'

'No, don't bother. I'll be leaving in a couple of minutes or so anyway, so I'll see to it.'

Maggie smiled. 'Bye, then. See you tomorrow.'

Jaimie tidied her desk, reached for her bag and coat and took one last look round the room, before making her way through to the office.

Switching off the light, she went into Reception

and came to an abrupt halt as she saw a man standing at the desk. He was in his early twenties, she guessed. Thin and pale, he had several days' growth of stubble on his chin. His hair was long and lank.

Her heart gave an extra thud.

'Oh, you startled me. I thought everyone had gone.' She glanced at her watch and smiled. 'Look, I'm sorry but the surgery is closed. Did you have an appointment?'

He dug his hands in the pockets of his jackets. 'Yeah, that's right.' He moved away slightly, letting his glance flit in desultory fashion round the room. 'This is nice, very nice. I'm impressed.' His gaze lingered with undisguised interest on her knee-length skirt and the neat polo-necked sweater.

'Yes.' She moved behind the desk in an attempt to thwart the blatantly lingering gaze and found herself battling with a sudden feeling of unease.

'You're new here.'

'Yes.' She moistened her lips with her tongue. 'I'm acting as locum for Dr Reynolds until he's well enough to return to work.'

He nodded. 'I've seen you around.' He moved towards the desk. 'I didn't realise you closed early today or I'd have got here sooner.' His gaze narrowed. 'Are you alone?'

Her own gaze flickered as she experienced a fresh sense of panic. 'Not for long.' She watched him warily. She didn't know this man from Adam. She certainly wasn't about to volunteer that sort of information to a stranger.

For all she knew he could be a burglar...or worse! She frowned. 'Dr Paige should be back any minute now. He has to collect his diary and list of visits.'

Jaimie found herself wishing desperately that Sam would walk through the door. He would know what to do. But he didn't.

She looked at the clock on the wall. 'Actually, he's late.' She frowned. 'You *did* say you had an appointment?'

Her glance flickered towards the phone. If only she could get to it. With an effort she managed to smile. 'Perhaps I can look it up for you. There may have been a mistake. What did you say the name was? I'll just give our secretary a call…'

She reached for the phone but he intercepted her, his hand resting over hers. He looked suddenly uneasy. 'It's, er…Jessop.'

'Jessop.' She frowned, leafing through the diary. 'No, I don't see it. Look, I'll just make that call. I'm sure there must have been a mistake.'

'No. Don't do that.' He gave a short laugh. 'Hey, look, don't worry about it. It's my fault. I was supposed to pick up my gran. She was seeing the nurse. Yeah, that's it, the nurse. I must have got the day wrong or something.'

He tugged at the zip of his jacket and backed towards the door. 'Yeah, that'll be it.'

He departed and Jaimie was left staring at the door. Her heart was still thudding as she collected her keys, locked the doors and finally headed thankfully towards her car.

But for some reason even the cottage didn't seem to offer the usual welcome when she returned to it, probably because the fire had died down, leaving a distinct chill in the air, and the debris from various cups of coffee still littered the kitchen. It was definitely turning out to be one of those days.

Sighing, she abandoned her coat and set about reviving the fire, which soon flickered into life again, before she switched on the kettle and ran upstairs to change into a comfortable pair of jeans and a sweatshirt.

She tied a scarf over her hair, before going downstairs to begin a vigorous and totally unnecessary assault upon the furniture with polish and duster.

The faint glimmering of the late afternoon sun had long since gone, and the air struck with a deepening chill before she finally perched on a kitchen stool to eat a hasty snack of beans on toast.

Eyeing the plate with a distinct lack of enthusiasm, she forced the food down, and was just carrying the plate to the sink when the doorbell rang.

Frowning, she glanced at the clock. Now, who on earth could that be? It was probably Giles. No one else knew she was home, but the smile she was wearing vanished instantly as she opened the door, gasping as it let in a blast of cold air.

She felt her heart miss a beat. Sam stood there. Flakes of snow had settled in his hair. Faded jeans hugged his lean hips and thighs and he looked very, very desirable. She felt her hackles rise, along with her defences.

'Oh, it's you,' she snapped uncharitably.

He returned her stare, a flicker of amusement briefly twisting his mouth, and her hand flew to the scarf covering her hair. She dragged it off roughly, leaving her curls flattened and dishevelled.

She probably had a smut on her nose, too, because he was looking at her with the kind of critical appraisal that left her blushing and wishing she had at least taken the time to put on a smear of lipstick.

She purposely made no attempt to invite him in, even when he glanced up at the leaden sky. It gave her a perverse kind of satisfaction to see him shiver and turn up the collar of his coat. He looked like a bedraggled puppy, she thought, and it served him right.

He was clutching a package—a plant, judging from the sodden paper which was slowly beginning to disintegrate in his hands. A present for Miss Forbes? Poison ivy, no doubt.

The thought flickered ungenerously through her mind as she said briskly, 'You won't mind if I don't invite you in, will you? Only I'm trying to catch on some chores, and I really don't have time to stand and chat.' She shivered. 'Besides, it's freezing out there.'

'I know the feeling. It must be about five below out here.' He peered over her shoulder to where the fire blazed, and a vague spasm of guilt ran through her as melting snow dripped from his hair. 'It looks cosy…and warm.'

'Yes, it is. Except when the door is wide open.'

He coughed.

She eyed him warily, sighed, then stepped back. 'I suppose you'd better come in,' she said ungraciously, leading him through to the sitting room. 'Now, is there something I can do for you, or is this simply a continuation of this morning's unpleasantries? Because, if so, to quote your own words, I object to mixing my business and social life.'

One dark eyebrow rose. 'Coffee would be nice.'

'Coffee is not on offer. I'm far too—'

The plant was waved under her nose. 'This is for you.'

She stared at it, and at him. His voice was husky. His eyes were sunk into their sockets and his features were taut with cold.

'For me? You're saying this is for me?' She held it at arm's length, eyeing the greenery suspiciously. 'Is this some kind of joke?'

He held the collar of his jacket tightly against his throat and she noticed that his hands were shaking. 'No joke. It was the only way I could think to apologise.' He frowned. 'Oh, God, you're not allergic, are you?'

'No.' Not to plants anyway. Arrogant men, they were altogether a different proposition.

'Well, thank goodness for that.' His mouth twisted slightly. 'Look, I really do apologise for the things I said this morning. I know they were unjustified. I can only offer this damned migraine as an excuse. I was feeling lousy. Still am for that matter.'

'You look awful.'

'Thank you. You say the nicest things.'

He was leaning against the door, his eyes closed, and she had to dart out a hand to steady him as he swayed. To her consternation she could feel the heat of his body burning even through his sodden clothes.

'For heaven's sake, Sam, you're burning with fever.'

'I feel cold.' His weight rested almost fully upon her now. In desperation she dropped the plant onto a nearby table and struggled to help him towards the couch.

'You are an idiot, Sam. Why didn't you say something? I suppose you do realise you have the flu?'

He looked at her with eyes that didn't quite seem

to focus and she was alarmed to feel him shaking violently.

'I always…seem…to say the wrong thing. Always end up fighting.' He closed his eyes again and she saw the beads of sweat on his face. 'God, Jaimie, I'm sorry. I feel awful. Don't think I can…make it.'

'Here, lean on me.' She gasped as he took her at her word.

Somehow she managed to manoeuvre him onto the couch where he collapsed, sitting with a hand flung over his eyes.

She thought for one awful moment that he had passed out.

'Sam?'

'Sorry.' He drew a deep, rasping breath. 'Can't think what—'

'Don't talk. I'm going to try to make you more comfortable. Let me help you off with your coat and shoes.'

He protested as she knelt and tried to ease off his shoes. 'Jaimie, you don't have to do this. Got to go. Just give me a minute.'

Grimly she eased him out of his jacket. 'Somehow I don't think you'll be going anywhere, not for a while yet anyway.'

He was a dead weight as she struggled to release him from the jacket, but finally she managed it and reproached herself as she carried it, dripping, into the kitchen and hung it over a chair. 'And you'll probably get pneumonia as well, thanks to me.'

Anger with herself turned to dismay as she returned to the sitting room to find him lying full length on the couch. He had tugged off his tie and his shirt was open at the neck. His hair, dampened by snow, was flattened against his head.

Without thinking, she bent to brush it back, and gasped softly as some powerful emotion surged through her like an electric current.

Biting at her lip, she straightened up and looked at the recumbent figure. 'This is all very well, Doctor, but just what am I supposed to do with you now?'

He didn't answer. She didn't expect him to. He was sleeping like a baby, snoring gently, and from the look of things was likely to stay that way for several hours.

'Oh. Great!' she muttered as she flopped into the chair opposite and sat watching the sleeping figure. 'This is all I need.'

It suddenly occurred to her that it was odd that she hadn't been able to visualise Giles in the cottage, completing a picture of domestic bliss, and yet now, for some inexplicable reason, it was as if the missing piece of a jigsaw had suddenly slipped into place.

Jaimie studied Sam. He looked different when he was asleep. Younger, more vulnerable somehow. As if Sam Paige could ever be vulnerable. She saw the faint lines around his eyes and mouth and wondered what had put them there. A woman perhaps? Helen Forbes?

The image was somehow strangely disturbing. She got to her feet, going into the kitchen to fill a hot-water bottle and to fetch a blanket as she waited for the kettle to boil.

There was only one thing wrong with this jigsaw puzzle. Someone kept coming along and changing the pieces, and just when she'd thought she had rebuilt it again it was only to discover that the most important piece of all was missing.

Her hands shook as she draped the blanket over him. As she did so he turned restlessly, groaning in his sleep, and without warning he reached out, imprisoning her hand and drawing her close.

She gasped and tried to pull away, only to feel his grip tighten so that she fell heavily against the couch. 'Don't go,' he muttered. 'Stay. Need you...'

Jaimie gritted her teeth. She was shocked to feel her eyes fill with tears. *Now* he needed her. But, then, she reasoned, he was delirious. He probably thought she was Helen.

She struggled with a protest but was silenced as his mouth suddenly closed warmly, demandingly, over hers.

This isn't fair, she thought. She could feel the powerful, muscular strength of him as he held her close. His kiss became more demanding. She could feel the passion build in him and gasped at the shaft of exquisite pleasure his touch sent coursing through her.

This was crazy. She should put a stop to it now, while there was still time.

For a moment, almost as if he sensed her hesitation, he became taut, then with a groan he drew her closer still until she had to force herself gently out of his grip to sit, breathing hard, on the floor beside him.

He was delirious, of course, didn't know what he was doing. Jaimie rested her head back against the couch and briefly closed her eyes. Sam moved restlessly. His hand came over her shoulder to rest gently against the fullness of her breast.

She drew a ragged breath, for some crazy reason feeling cheated. In the morning he wouldn't remember a thing about what had happened. Which was probably just as well.

The thought brought a faint blush to her cheeks and she released herself gently, moving to sit in the chair opposite. 'It's going to be a long night, Sam,' she said softly. It would be the first, the *only* night she would spend with him, and he wouldn't remember a thing about it.

Jaimie woke suddenly several hours later, and lay for a moment, trying to remember where she was. She felt cold and her neck ached where she had fallen asleep in the chair. But that wasn't what had woken her.

Her gaze flew to where Sam lay. The blanket had slipped to the floor and he was moaning restlessly with cold.

Alarmed, she got to her feet and regretted the hasty movements as the circulation began to return painfully to her limbs.

She put a hand on his forehead and was shocked to find him icy cold. He was probably uncomfortable, too. The couch wasn't built for someone over six feet tall.

Quickly she knelt before the fire, coaxing the dying embers back into life with a log. It started to crackle and the flickering light case shadows onto Sam's face.

He looked worse, she thought, with a fresh pang of concern, though, of course, it might have something to do with the fact that he needed a shave.

Jaimie found herself studying the shadowed planes of his face, made gentle by sleep, and with a sense of shock realised that she was within a hair's breadth of falling in love with this man! If she wasn't very careful it could happen. But there was no future in it, she reminded herself. He was already in love, with someone else.

It was several seconds before she realised that his eyes were open and that he was actually staring at her. Startled, she ran a hand through her hair, suddenly all too aware of how she must look.

Her eyes felt heavy from lack of sleep and for a moment she panicked. A few hours from now she was going to have to cope with morning surgery. Obviously she couldn't leave him alone.

'How can I explain you to the cleaning lady?' she murmured, biting at her lip. Then she remembered with a sigh of relief that it was the weekend.

'Thirsty.'

She was instantly wide awake, and hurried to the kitchen to fetch a glass of water and carry it, with a couple of aspirins, back to the sitting room where she found him struggling to retrieve the blankets.

Disentangling him, she helped him to sit up, supporting him gently as he sipped gratefully at the water.

'Here, you'd better take these with it. They'll help to bring your temperature down.'

He managed, with an effort, to swallow them, before falling back against the pillow and flinging one hand over his eyes. She knew by the heat of his body that he still had a fever, despite the fact that he was shivering.

'I'm sorry about this. I feel as weak as a kitten. I can't think what happened.'

Jaimie looked at him and smiled. 'Well, of course, I'm only a doctor, but I'd say you have a particularly nasty dose of flu. You must have been fighting it for days. Why on earth didn't you say anything?'

'Thought if I ignored it long enough it might go away.'

'Typical,' she snorted with disgust, wondering what it was about men that made them look so helpless when they were ill. 'You're supposed to be a doctor. Is that the sort of advice you'd give to one of your patients?'

Sam opened his eyes to look at her. 'Probably not.'

Her mouth compressed. 'You need taking in hand, Dr Paige.'

'Is that an offer? Because if so you've got the job.'

She blushed furiously. He was obviously still delirious, a belief confirmed as he started to shiver again.

'I'll get out of your way soon,' he muttered. 'I just feel so damned weak. Can't seem to get warm.'

He began tugging at the blanket. Jaimie gave a deep sigh. 'Somehow I get the feeling you won't be going anywhere for a while yet, Doctor.'

She prised it from his grasp, attempting to tuck it round him so that he couldn't throw it off again, but it was useless. Within seconds he turned and she found the blanket in a heap on the floor again.

'Look,' she sighed with exasperation and tiredness, 'you're not making things easy here. This is for your own good, Sam. If you think I'm going to see you catch pneumonia and end up as a guest in my spare bedroom, you've got another think coming. I don't need this kind of complication in my life, thank you very much.'

She draped the blanket over him again, tucking it in firmly with a hint of triumph, then gasped as the breath was knocked out of her as his hand shot out.

'I'm losing patience here, Sam.'

He shivered. 'Cold.'

She gritted her teeth. 'This is your last chance.' She advanced with the blanket, leaned forward to tuck it round his shoulders and suddenly found herself grasped in a bear-like hug.

She let out a screech of protest and tried to detach herself, feeling his unshaven chin rasp her face.

'Mmm, nice. Soft and warm.' Then he sighed and relaxed.

Jaimie lowered her head, tears of exhaustion and a whole mixture of pent-up emotions flooding through her as she lay like a doll in his arms.

'I'm fighting a losing battle here, aren't I?' She sniffed hard. 'Oh, what the heck. If this is the only way we're going to get any sleep around here...'

She lay on the edge of the couch beside him, conscious of the weight of his arm thrown across her. It was uncomfortable, but she stretched her legs out, scarcely daring to breathe as she tugged at the blanket.

'I can't believe I'm doing this,' she muttered into the darkness. Sam breathed steadily, warmly, into her ear.

She had just closed her eyes, forcing herself to breathe deeply and relax, when he flung the blanket off and she felt herself being dragged towards him.

Her heart thudded riotously as he moulded her body against his own. She couldn't move. Slowly his hand explored the soft roundness of her body beneath the shirt she was wearing and she gasped with indignation. Then he muttered something and lay still.

Trapped beneath the arm he had flung over her, Jaimie lay staring into the darkness, breathing hard and feeling the tears prick at her eyes until, finally, she remonstrated with herself aloud.

'Oh, for heaven's sake, go to sleep. You're not likely to get ravished on your own couch, and even if you did, let's face it, he's not likely to remember anything about it.'

She gulped hard and licked away the tear that slid down her cheek, not knowing whether to laugh or cry. Life was full of frustrations.

CHAPTER TEN

IT WAS daylight when Jaimie woke again. She felt warm—too warm—and there was a gentle, whistling sound in her ear.

She turned her head warily to glance at the tousled head beside her, and felt her throat tighten. Sam looked younger, more vulnerable somehow now that the fever had finally broken.

'And good morning to you, too,' she muttered, firmly resisting the urge to brush back the hair from his eyes.

She left him sleeping and crept into the kitchen to flip the switch on the electric kettle, before going upstairs to shower and change her clothes.

Five minutes later she was back in the kitchen, making coffee and toast, when she heard a sharp exclamation and, going to the doorway, saw Sam sitting up.

He raked a hand through his hair, surveying himself and his surroundings with total bewilderment. There was something ridiculously childlike about the way he sat with the blanket tucked over his knees.

A cloud of smoke alerted her to the burning toast. 'Oh, no!' She flew to rescue it, gazed in dismay at the charred remains and dropped it crossly into the bin.

Sam rubbed at his eyes and the growth of stubble on his chin as she emerged from the kitchen with a

139

mug of coffee, which she handed to him. 'Here, drink this. It will help.'

He gazed down at the steaming liquid, took a long, satisfying drink and said huskily, 'What the hell is going on? How did I get here?'

She sat on the chair opposite, cupped her hands round her own mug of coffee and tried to ignore the fact that he was naked from the waist up.

A pulse began to hammer at the base of her throat. 'You've been ill. Don't you remember?'

'Can't say I do.' He took another sip of his coffee and looked round the room. 'Why here?'

She smiled slightly. 'You arrived on the doorstep, clutching a plant—by way of an apology, I think you said. After which you collapsed. I toyed with the idea of sending for an ambulance and having you taken to hospital, but you seemed to have other plans.'

She nodded in the direction of the couch. 'You fell asleep and I hadn't the heart to throw you out.' Which is what I should have done if I'd had any sense, she thought.

He groaned, gulped at his coffee as if it might clear his senses and looked at her. 'I don't know what to say. I'm sorry. I must have caused you a lot of—'

'Trouble?' She smiled sweetly.

It was an understatement if ever she'd heard one, Jaimie thought as she rushed into the kitchen to rescue the second lot of toast. She called to him through the open door, 'Forget it. I coped. Besides, it wasn't your fault.'

He didn't answer and when she returned he was on his feet, even if it did look as if he regretted the action.

'I'd take it easy if I were you,' she prompted.

'You're probably over the worst but I wouldn't do anything too hasty.'

He groaned and pressed a hand to his head. 'I don't think there's much chance of that. I feel as weak as a kitten.'

Remembering his strength last night, she chose to ignore that. 'You should eat something. Toast, perhaps, or I could rustle up some bacon and—'

She broke off as he stared with dawning horror at the blanket he was clutching, and his clothes—or rather lack of them.

'My clothes! Where are my clothes?' He stared at her. 'You didn't? Tell me you didn't?'

She gave a hoot of laughter. 'Oh, come on, Sam. I am a doctor, for heaven's sake. I've seen a man's body before.'

'Not mine you haven't,' he growled. His blue eyes glinted. 'You're enjoying this, aren't you?'

With an effort she managed not to laugh. 'Absolutely not,' she said primly. 'Besides, I simply removed your shirt and trousers because you were running a high temperature, and to make you more comfortable. You have my word—you're perfectly decent.' And utterly desirable.

She swallowed hard as with a strangled cry of indignation he dragged the blanket more securely round his waist.

'I've imposed on your hospitality long enough,' Sam ground out. 'I need a shower and a shave then I'll get out of your way.'

Easier said than done, she thought. And he needn't have said it with quite so much enthusiasm. She bit at her lip. 'Help yourself. The bathroom is upstairs. Your clothes are on a hanger in the bedroom. I'll be in the kitchen. If you need anything, shout.' She turned away.

He paused. 'Jaimie, wait.' He brushed a hand through his hair. 'Look, I'm sorry. I really am grateful. It's just that... Hell, I know I'm not saying this very well.'

'You don't need to say anything.' She kept her response purposely light, almost flippant, and was glad to be able to give her attention to scrambling eggs while he went upstairs to shower and dress.

She swallowed hard. It was ridiculous but suddenly she hated the thought of seeing him walk out of the door, hated the thought of the emptiness after he had gone. Making breakfast for two was a habit she could get to like. She had a momentary vision of doing it for the rest of her life. And of lying in his arms...

The memories came flooding back and she gave a yelp as he was suddenly behind her, very close, his hands on her shoulders.

'I don't blame you for being angry.'

She turned and almost wished she hadn't as the sensual mouth loomed closer. 'I'm not angry. Why should I be? You didn't ask to be ill.'

'Maybe not.' His eyes searched her face far too intently for her comfort. 'All the same, we didn't exactly get off to a good start, did we? And I didn't make things any easier. The last thing you needed was to have me turn up, unannounced, spending the night on the couch.'

He frowned and she looked away from the questions she saw beginning to form in his mind.

'I told you, it was no trouble.' She rushed to forestall him. 'You slept like a baby most of the time.'

She tried to ease herself away but, infuriatingly, his

grip tightened fractionally on her arm. She followed his gaze through the doorway to the chair where the cushions were still piled up as she had left them.

She saw a thoughtful expression edge its way into his eyes as if he was trying to remember.

'And how about you?'

'Me?' She gave a slight laugh and felt the warm colour surge into her cheeks. 'What about me?'

His glittering gaze was suddenly brooding. 'You can't have got much sleep last night.'

'I managed. Anyway, I don't need much sleep.'

He looked at the chair again, and suddenly there was a hint of laughter in his eyes. 'That can't have been very comfortable.'

'It was fine.' She swallowed hard. 'It's a large chair.' Why did she sound so breathless?

His dark eyebrows rose. 'And you're not exactly large, are you, Jaimie? In fact, you wouldn't take up much room at all, would you?' he said huskily.

She found her gaze drawn to the firm line of his jaw, the sensual mouth and the blue eyes which seemed to be having a strangely hypnotic effect on her.

She knew he was laughing at her and before she could guess his intention he had drawn her slowly towards him. His glittering gaze narrowed briefly and the choking sound in her throat died as his mouth closed slowly, possessively, over hers.

Don't do this to me, Sam, she thought. Right now my resistance is very, very low. I can't play games. Her pulse rate accelerated dangerously, and she closed her eyes.

The effect of his nearness was creating an intensity

of sexual awareness she had never experienced before.

'We should do this more often,' he said softly against her ear.

'I don't think that's a good idea,' she told him breathlessly, tilting her head up to look at him.

It was a mistake. For an instant she felt him tense, then he bent his head and his mouth swooped again to take gentle possession of her lips. The effect was devastating. It left her feeling confused and shaken. The fact that he drew away, staring at her before releasing her gently, left her feeling irrationally depressed.

'I think it's time I left.'

She blinked hard on the tears that threatened to well up. 'But you haven't eaten anything.'

His gaze swept her face. 'I'm not really hungry, thanks. Besides, I've a lot of catching up to do.'

'Yes.' With Miss Forbes, no doubt. She nodded, unable to speak. Suddenly she felt exhausted. 'I think it's time I did some work too.' She looked around the room and knew it would never seem the same again. There would be too many memories.

'I'm afraid I've upset your routine.'

Far more than her routine, she thought. 'It doesn't matter.' A voice in her retaliated crossly. Yes it does. You stroll into my life, Sam, turn it upside down and then walk away, leaving me to pick up the pieces.

With an effort she forced a smile and he studied her reflectively. 'I'm sorry if I kept you from anything important.'

With a gasp of horror her hand flew to her mouth as she remembered she had promised to phone Giles. 'Oh no…'

'I take it that means I did.' There was a sudden note of coolness in his voice. 'I seem to keep apologising, but I imagine you'll be able to put things right.'

He was already gathering up his jacket. 'I'll be going and let you do whatever you have to do.'

She watched him walk out to his car and drive away before she returned to the kitchen. She stared with disgust at the pan of congealed eggs and felt the tears prick at her eyes as she shovelled them into the bin.

'Damn!' Her hand shook as she reached for the kettle and made herself a strong cup of tea and loaded it with sugar, before carrying it into the sitting room where she sat on the couch.

It was still warm and instinctively she pulled the blanket round her. She sipped at her tea then grimaced and got to her feet. 'I don't even like having tea first thing in the morning.'

She caught sight of her reflection in the mirror. There were shadows beneath her eyes and she was pale. 'But, then, I don't do a lot of things,' she told herself faintly. 'Or, at least, I didn't.'

A flush stole into her cheeks. She walked briskly into the kitchen and spent the rest of the morning trying to erase all trace of Sam from her mind as well as the cottage.

CHAPTER ELEVEN

MONDAY morning came around far too soon. Driving to the surgery, Jaimie found herself dreading the inevitable meeting with Sam. Not that he was likely to have remembered the events of the weekend any more clearly, she comforted herself. If only she could erase them from her own mind so easily.

She felt irritable and tired and, worse, looked it. Giles had commented on it when he'd come round for a drink the previous night, and she'd heard herself reluctantly telling him, without elaborating too much, what had happened.

'He just arrived on the doorstep, handed me a plant and more or less passed out. I had no choice but to let him stay. It's this damned flu. Half our patients are down with it.'

'Poor old thing. You should have told me. I wouldn't have suggested coming over for a drink.'

She'd wanted sympathy and she'd got it. That was the nice thing about Giles, she'd thought, snuggling up to him on the couch, her head resting on his chest. He was uncomplicated and predictable. Dear, safe, reliable Giles. Who wanted excitement anyway? She'd had enough of it to last a lifetime.

He'd brushed a wisp of hair from her cheek and smiled down at her. 'I found another picture. I want you to have it, a present from me. It'll look nice over there with the others.'

Guilt had reared its ugly head. 'Oh, Giles, you're so nice. I'm sorry I'm such awful company tonight.'

He'd looked at her and smiled. 'You're never awful company. I love being with you, you know that. But you do look tired. I hope you're not going down with a dose of flu as well.'

'I'll be fine. I just need an early night, that's all.'

And she had done just that after he'd left. But it hadn't helped. She had woken after a restless sleep, feeling cross and even more tired.

In the event she needn't have worried anyway, because Sam had arrived at the surgery only seconds ahead of her. He was just getting out of his car as she turned her own vehicle onto the drive.

It was too early in the day for a confrontation. Instead, she made a play of foraging in her bag, hoping he would go in ahead of her. But just when she thought the coast was clear he turned back to collect something from the back seat, and as he straightened up their eyes locked before he slammed the door and strode away.

He was wearing a dark suit. He still looked tired and pale and Jaimie found herself wondering whether Helen was a good cook and, if so, why she didn't give him a good square meal. Then she reminded herself firmly that their domestic arrangements were none of her business.

He was holding the door open a little impatiently when she finally locked her car and ran up the steps.

'Thanks.' She hurried through into the warmth and felt his arm brush against her sleeve.

It was ridiculous, the effect that even so minor a contact had on her, yet Sam's expression didn't change. There wasn't even the merest flicker of a smile. That, in a way, was comforting, because it seemed to confirm that he hadn't remembered any more. Even so, she was annoyed to find that her own cheeks were suddenly warm.

'I didn't expect to see you back so soon.' Her voice was even more brisk than she had intended and his brows rose. Surely that couldn't be laughter she saw in his eyes?

'Thanks for the concern. I didn't know you cared.' His eyes looked directly into hers and, to her chagrin, it was she who looked away.

'It's just nice to know I don't have to cover both surgeries,' she blustered. 'You were quite ill. I thought you might need a couple of days in bed…' She floundered helplessly as his gaze fixed itself on her.

'Now, there's a nice thought. Unfortunately, I don't think it's justified. I'm fine, thanks to your efforts. I slept most of yesterday.' His gaze narrowed. 'I don't know if I thanked you properly.'

She stared with agonised concentration at the buttons on her jacket. 'Yes, you did. Look, I must go. I need to make a few phone calls before I see my first patient.'

'Same here. Oh, by the way, this is for you.' He handed her an envelope.

She took it, recognising Jon's handwriting.

'It's an invitation, for tomorrow evening.'

'Invitation?'

'I've had one too. Jon likes to get everyone together on a social level every now and again so that we can chat and exchange views without being too formal.' He smiled. 'It's usually a good evening. I'm looking forward to it.'

'You mean we're both…?'

'We're both invited, yes. But not together if that's what's worrying you.' There was sudden tension in his voice. 'You can bring a guest. I don't imagine that will present too many problems.'

She might have said the same of him, Jaimie thought. She toyed briefly with the idea of making some excuse and refusing the invitation, but knew she couldn't do it. Apart from anything else, it would be unfair to Jon.

'I don't think we should disappoint Jon. He's had a pretty rough time of it lately. He could do with some kind of diversion right now.'

She nodded, slightly unnerved by his apparent ability to read her thoughts. 'I'll telephone him later. Oh, but what about covering here? We can't both be off duty.'

'It's not a problem. We can get any calls transferred to one of the local GPs. It's a reciprocal arrangement. We cover for each other. Besides, if there's any real emergency I can always be reached on my mobile.'

'Oh, well, that's fine.' But as she walked away Jaimie had the distinct feeling that somehow she had been out-manoeuvred.

She telephoned Giles who, as she expected, greeted the idea with enthusiasm. 'Yes, I'd love to come. It will be nice to see Jon again and any excuse to spend an evening with you, even if we won't be alone, is great. I shall look forward to it. Pick you up at eight?'

Jaimie smiled. 'Yes, that's fine. I shall look forward to it too.'

Giles laughed. 'Not exactly a night off for you,

though, is it? Poor darling. I mean, you must see enough of Sam during the day.'

'I expect I'll bear up. He's really not that bad, you know, in small doses.'

'I'll take your word for it.' Giles's laugh echoed her own. 'See you tomorrow, then.'

'Till tomorrow.'

She made her way into Reception. The waiting room was already full.

'It's a cold morning out there.' Maggie looked up, smiling, as she made an entry in the diary and then handed over the morning mail. 'These are for you.'

'I know. It's freezing.' Chafing her hands, Jaimie accepted the pile of letters and patients' cards. 'All for me?' She smiled wryly.

'Afraid so. It's like Waterloo station out there. The rush started early.'

'I'd better make a start, then. We don't want a mutiny on our hands. Oh, by the way...' Jaimie hesitated. 'I don't suppose a Mrs Jessop has been in?'

'Jessop.' Maggie frowned. 'Not that I remember. Mind you, if I was in the office Paula may have seen her. I can always check.'

Jaimie shook her head. 'No, don't worry. It's not important. I probably got the name wrong anyway.'

She made her way to her consulting room and rang the bell for her first patient, wondering what Helen was likely to wear the following evening and mentally assessing the contents of her own wardrobe. It was beginning to become a habit.

In the event she chose a trouser suit in soft black fabric. Beneath the loose jacket she wore a camisole, and a fine gold chain and earrings emphasised the colour of her hair and eyes.

She had gone to endless pains, shampooing her hair and applying a touch of make-up to her face. The results justified the effort if Giles's reaction was anything to go by as she answered the door.

His hands lingered on her shoulders as he brushed a kiss against her cheek. 'You look gorgeous. So gorgeous, in fact, that I'm seriously beginning to wish we didn't have to go out. I'd much rather have you all to myself.'

'You always say the nicest things.' She smiled as she returned his kiss. The thought that he was going to be beside her at Uncle Jon's gave her a comfortable feeling so that she relaxed.

'It's very easy to say nice things about you,' Giles murmured. As if sensing a change in her, his kiss became more demanding. He drew a breath and looked at her. 'Oh, Jaimie, have you any idea how I feel about you?' He kissed her again.

It was if their relationship had suddenly moved into a new phase. The knowledge left her feeling confused and she managed to evade him light-heartedly as he pulled her closer again. 'This is very nice but hadn't we better go? We're due at Jon's in half an hour.'

'I suppose you're right.' Giles released her with obvious reluctance. 'I just want to be sure you know how I feel about you, that's all.'

'I think I do,' she said softly.

'Oh, damn, why do we have to go out? There's so much I want to say to you.'

'Because I promised and they're expecting us.' She smiled gently. It was a relief to get into the car where she could sit in the darkness and be alone with her thoughts, if only for a little while.

Sam and Helen had arrived at the house before

them. Jaimie heard their voices through the open door and caught a glimpse of Sam, standing with a glass in his hand, beside the girl who smiled up at him.

Helen looked staggeringly attractive in a simple, figure-hugging dress. With a pang, Jaimie noticed how attractive Sam looked in the dark suit.

For a moment, as she stood in the hallway, his gaze rose to hers and her heart thudded. Then Giles's hand was gently urging her forward and Jon was inviting them in and offering them drinks.

'Jaimie, my dear. I'm so glad you could come— and Giles.'

'It's good to see you, too, Uncle Jon. But should you being doing this?'

'I'm fine, my dear. Thoroughly enjoying myself. The food's all under control in the kitchen,' he reassured her, smiling as he kissed her cheek. 'There's time for an aperitif. What will you have?'

'Sherry, please. Dry.' She looked at Giles. 'I think I'd better just tidy up first. You go in. I'll join you in a minute.'

She fled to the bathroom, closed the door and leaned against it, breathing hard. This was ridiculous. Her legs were shaking. There was a whole evening to get through. Somehow she was going to have to chat and be polite, and pretend that her heart wasn't breaking every time she looked across the table and saw Sam, gazing into the eyes of the woman he loved.

I can't do it, she thought, battling against a feeling of panic. It was crazy. Everything was getting out of hand.

She drew a ragged breath. Somehow she had to pull herself together and get through the evening. After that… She left the question unanswered because right then she didn't have any answers.

They were all talking animatedly when she returned to the lounge. Helen and Giles were engaged in a deep conversation and Jon excused himself on the pretext of seeing what progress was being made in the kitchen.

'You'll get Jaimie her drink, won't you, my boy?'

Sam came to her side moments later and handed her a glass. 'One dry sherry.'

She took it, careful to avoid any physical contact, and sipped at it. Sam's gaze followed hers.

'Jon's looking better, isn't he?'

'Yes, I thought so, too. I was afraid it might be my imagination—seeing what I wanted to see.' In spite of herself she turned to look at him. 'Were my thoughts so obvious?'

'Only to me,' he said gravely. 'But, then, I imagine we're both worried, both looking for the same thing.'

If only that were true, she thought. They moved towards the fire. Helen's gaze rose above Giles's shoulder and Jaimie noticed that her face briefly lost its animated look, her expression changing to one of faint displeasure. But if he noticed there was no sign of it on Sam's face.

'Do you think we're in danger of being over-optimistic—about Jon, I mean?' She knew she was talking too quickly but at least this was safe ground.

'There's no way of knowing. I hope not. He knows he has to be reasonable.'

She laughed. 'I'm not sure Jon understands reasonable.'

'You could be right.' His voice softened as he looked at her. 'You love him very much, don't you?'

'Yes, I do.' She couldn't prevent the sudden tightening in her throat.

'Well, as it happens, so do I. He's been almost like a father at times. Always there when I needed him. So I do know what you're going through.'

'I just don't want anything to happen to him.'

'Then we won't let it, will we?' His hand closed firmly over hers. She closed her eyes, then the glass was eased gently from her fingers. Her eyes flew open.

'You need to eat.'

It was a statement, not a question. In fact, she hadn't eaten, but what right had he to know her so well? Her skin warmed under his heated, lingering gaze and she said on a flustered note, 'Lead me to it. I'm starving.'

His hand came down under her arm and her heart performed a crazy little dance. It faded to a dull bump as Giles came towards her and she found herself relinquished almost too quickly into his care.

For the rest of the evening she sat opposite Sam, who seemed effortlessly to direct the flow of conversation and easy laughter without noticing that she didn't manage to eat much after all.

They adjourned for coffee and Jaimie couldn't help noticing that he didn't seem to mind in the least the proprietorial manner in which Helen linked her arm through his, as if staking her claim.

Jaimie turned her attention to Giles, beaming at him, and suddenly realised guiltily that she hadn't heard a word he'd been saying for the past two minutes.

'Do go through to the sitting room,' Jon directed. 'I'll be with you in a minute. Sam, I know I've a rather special bottle of brandy somewhere. Damned if I can find it. Help me look for it, there's a good chap.'

Helen followed them in their search for the elusive bottle. Giles led Jaimie to the sitting room which was suffused by the glow from the fire and a solitary lamp. It was cosy, smelling of old books and wax polish.

A tray of coffee had been left on one of the tables. Jaimie moved towards it, purposely avoiding looking at the clock, wondering how long it would be before she could reasonably make an excuse to leave.

The meal had been lovely and cooked to perfection, yet somehow it had tasted like chaff in her mouth.

'Sugar? Cream?'

'Later.' Giles was behind her. He drew her gently away from it and took her in his arms. 'Coffee can wait. Right now I've more important things on my mind. I just want to kiss you and tell you how beautiful you are.'

Giles took the coffee-pot from her, putting it onto the tray. He really was quite attractive in a nice, gentle sort of way, Jaimie found herself thinking. Not like Sam's rugged good looks, of course. But, then, not every woman went for the macho type, she tried to reason with herself crossly, allowing herself to be kissed.

Her head was aching and she felt a little light-headed. Probably because she had drunk more than she would normally have done because toying with the glass had seemed like the perfect ploy to cover the fact that she wasn't eating.

She was beginning to realise it might have been a mistake and let her head rest against Giles's chest until the slight feeling of queasiness passed. Sam had been right, damn him. She should have eaten a proper lunch.

She became aware that Giles was manoeuvring her face up to his and kissing her with a thoroughness that took her by surprise. It was a pleasant sensation, she decided, but it lacked the power to rouse her as Sam had been able to do.

My God, she thought, stifling a giggle. I'm assessing them as if they were bottles of wine.

Her hands pushed gently at Giles's chest as she came up for air.

'I love you, Jaimie, you know that, don't you?' His voice was muffled against her hair. 'I've known since the day we met that there was something very special about you and the way I feel for you. Well, the second time we met anyway. On the first I was a little hazy.'

He raised her face between his hands and kissed her again.

'Giles, I…' The room was spinning and she felt oddly disappointed that it was the effects of the wine rather than the kiss. Perhaps if she closed her eyes and pretended it was Sam… Her mouth quivered. She felt Giles's momentary surprise before he responded, this time more fiercely.

'Jaimie, oh, Jaimie,' he murmured huskily. 'I do love you. Say you'll marry me.'

The bubble burst. She moaned softly, knowing that she was only fooling herself that anyone could ever take Sam's place. Then she became dimly aware, as her eyes flew open, of the figure standing in the doorway.

The disbelief in Sam's eyes turned to mockery and then contempt as he took in her flushed cheeks and the glazed look in her eyes.

He thinks I'm drunk, she thought. She struggled to free herself from Giles's embrace, conscious only of Sam's stony expression. It was all too obvious he had drawn his own conclusions.

'Forgive me.' His voice was icy. 'I've obviously chosen the wrong moment to intrude.'

'Sam, I...' She tried to explain but it was too late. He was already turning on his heel and was gone.

Desolation washed over her. She wondered how long he had been standing there. Obviously long enough to have heard Giles's proposal.

White-faced, she pressed a hand to her head. Reaching out, she found a chair and flopped into it, closing her eyes. 'I'm so sorry, Giles. You were saying something...'

He smiled wryly. 'Actually, I was proposing, but I seem to have managed to get my timing all wrong, haven't I?'

She opened her eyes and with an effort managed to smile. 'It isn't your fault. Giles, I really do have the most awful headache. Would you mind very much if I asked you to take me home?'

He was instantly all concern. 'My poor darling, you do look a bit peaky. Perhaps it's this flu that's going around. Yes, of course I'll take you home. I'll just have a word with Jon. Will you be all right while I get your coat?'

She nodded. 'I'm afraid Sam didn't look too pleased.'

'It's hardly our fault that he chose to walk in at the wrong moment.'

She tried miserably to convince herself that it hadn't been quite as bad as she'd imagined, but knew that it had. Her cheeks had been flushed, her eyes too bright, and he must have been sickeningly aware of the ecstasy in her eyes. But there was no way she could explain, even if he gave her the chance, that it had been him she'd been thinking of, not Giles.

'I suppose you're right,' she agreed numbly.

'Besides, Sam does have a bit of a chip on his shoulder about that sort of thing. Not really surprising, I suppose. It's probably all to do with that girl he was engaged to.'

Jaimie felt her scalp tingle. 'Sam was...engaged?'

'Of course, I forgot, you probably wouldn't know about that. Yes, he was engaged to a girl. As far as I know, they'd planned the wedding and then about a month before it actually happened she became ill. I'm not sure exactly what the problem was, but she died. It was all very sudden. I don't know all the details but Sam took it very hard. I don't think he's ever got over it properly.'

Jaimie felt pity flood through her as she struggled to get to her feet, fighting the dull headache which had begun to pound in her skull. She swallowed hard. 'I had no idea.'

'No, well, I don't suppose there's any reason why you should. It's not something he talks about.' Giles frowned. 'Look, I think I'd better get you home. You look awful.'

He went in search of Jon. She heard the brief exchange of words, then she was being ushered out of the door into the cold night air, with words of concern and reassurance ringing in her ears.

From the car she looked back. Sam was standing in the doorway. It needed an effort of will not to get out of the car and fling herself into his arms.

Then another figure came to stand beside him,

small, slender. She reached up to say something then, together, they turned and went back into the house, closing the door behind them.

Jaimie was glad Giles made no attempt to come into the cottage. 'Get some sleep. Have a nice warm drink. I'll call you in the morning. Not too early.'

She managed a smile and her lips brushed his cheek. 'Dear Giles, I really am sorry. I've spoiled your evening.'

'Nonsense. I love being with you.'

Her head was still aching as she undressed and finally collapsed into bed. She swallowed two aspirins then switched out the light. She hadn't expected to sleep, but her last thought was of Sam's face as he'd stood in the doorway with Helen beside him.

CHAPTER TWELVE

WITH a little careful organisation Jaimie managed to avoid seeing Sam the next morning.

It had taken a real effort to drag herself out of bed and when she'd peered into the mirror she'd wished she hadn't. Her face had been pale, and even a brave flourish with her lipstick had done little to disguise the fact that she'd been feeling decidedly frail.

Surgery was busier than usual and she emerged feeling wrung out to drink a cup of coffee in the staff-room, grateful that Sam had been called out and that she wouldn't have to face him yet awhile.

Ruth came through from Reception to find her staring out of the window. Snow had given way to fine sleet and it was blowing in whirling gusts against the trees. Jaimie shivered at the thought of having to go out.

'You look awful.'

Ruth's voice intruded and Jaimie drew herself up with a start. 'Sorry, I was miles away.'

'I said are you all right. You look terrible. Perhaps you're coming down with this flu.'

'I shouldn't think so.' Jaimie managed to smile. 'I've just got a bit of a headache, that's all.' Nothing that wouldn't be put right by being in Sam's arms. The only trouble with that was that the particular cure wasn't on offer.

'I've promised myself a long, hot bath and an early night. That should do the trick.' Her glance went to the paper Ruth was carrying with rueful apprehension. 'That's not a call for me, is it?'

'I'm afraid so. Sorry about that. It came in a couple of minutes ago. It's young Nicky Witherspoon again.'

Jaimie sighed and read the details. 'I don't think it's too urgent. I've one other visit. I'll fit this one in on my way back to the surgery.' She glanced wryly at her watch. 'At this rate, that will be just about in time for evening surgery.'

Ruth picked up the empty coffee-cup, eyeing Jaimie's pale face with some concern. 'You really don't look well. I could always call Sam. I'm sure he'd do the visits for you.'

'No.' Jaimie frowned at the sharpness in her own voice, then smiled. 'Really, there's no need. He's busy enough as it is. Anyway, I'll pop back with these case notes later this afternoon then go straight home and have that early night.'

She got into her car and headed for the first of her calls, which turned out to be a child with a sore throat. By the time she was on her way to the second address the snow was coming down heavily and she was dismayed to find that it needed a real effort to keep the car steady on some of the narrower roads.

She was feeling thoroughly chilled. The car's windscreen wipers moved sluggishly under the weight of snow as it drifted towards her like huge moths picked out in the rapidly fading light.

It was almost a relief to pull up at the next house. She sat for a moment in the car, waiting for a spell of dizziness to pass before getting out and walking on legs which felt like rubber to the door.

She felt awful. Perhaps Ruth had been right and she was going down with flu after all.

Forty minutes later, back in the car, she rested her head on her arms against the steering-wheel for a minute, before forcing herself to concentrate. She passed a hand across her forehead and felt how hot it was. She needed a drink. Glancing at her watch, she decided there was just time to head back to the cottage to make herself a nice, comforting cup of hot chocolate and swallow some aspirins before heading back to the surgery.

Pulling into the drive, Jaimie climbed out of the car and fumbled in her bag for her keys as she made her way towards the front door of the cottage.

She paused for a moment, juggling the keys in her numbed fingers, then she froze. The door of the cottage was open, yet she was sure she had closed it. Something—someone—must be in there.

Easing the door fractionally open, she peered inside. It took a few seconds for her eyes to adjust to the darkness. There was no sign of movement.

Feeling her heart thudding in her chest, she took a wary step forward. Her mouth felt dry. She pushed carefully at the door of the sitting room and gasped at the scene that met her eyes.

Drawers had been pulled out and their contents scattered across the floor. Books and ornaments had been swept from the shelves.

Shakily, her fingers fumbled for the light switch, then wished she hadn't as everything seemed to spin crazily around her as she realised that someone—an intruder—must have been here, forced his way in.

Jaimie felt physically sick. She exhaled painfully, then froze as the sound of breaking glass drew her to the foot of the stairs and the numbing realisation that she wasn't alone.

Shock gave way to a new and even more powerful sensation as anger overrode fear and every other emotion at the realisation that he was still here, in the cottage, violating her privacy.

Her foot was on the stairs. Slowly she began to climb, peering into the semi-darkness. A thin shaft of light—she guessed from a torch—flickered. He was in the bedroom.

Halfway up the stairs, the board beneath her foot creaked. Jaimie heard a muffled exclamation, then suddenly above her, a figure loomed out of the darkness.

The breath snagged in her throat. In the next instant he was lunging towards her. She uttered a sharp cry as his weight crashed into her, slamming her against the wall.

For one crazy second she looked into his eyes, then she was falling. Her head made contact with something hard. Vaguely, Jaimie was aware that she screamed. A door slammed, then the floor rose up to meet her and she lay still.

When she opened her eyes again it was dark. She lay for several seconds, fighting the mists that seemed to be clogging her brain. Her head ached and she felt sick. What had happened? One minute she had been walking up the stairs and the next—

'Oh, no!' She groaned as dawning memory returned, bringing with it the vague realisation that a shaft of cold air was blowing in through the open door.

Warily she tried to move, groaning softly as pain shot through her head. Shakily her fingers rose to probe the ache at her temple, and she was shocked to feel a warm trickle of blood.

Carefully she sat up, waiting for a spell of dizziness to pass before slowly dragging herself to her feet. Her hand automatically fumbled for the light switch and turned it on. The action allayed a feeling of panic but it was only temporary.

She was alone, and it was dark outside. Suppose the intruder returned? Her head was spinning. She knew she wasn't capable of getting to the car and driving herself to the surgery. She would be a menace to herself and anyone else on the roads. But the thought of being here alone, all night...

Jaimie sat on the stairs, buried her aching head in her hands and sobbed, wishing Sam were there. Suddenly, as if in some uncanny way her thoughts had conjured him out of thin air, he was standing there, his face ashen and taut with anger as he gathered her into the blissful haven of his arms.

Of course it wasn't really happening, she told herself, making no effort to resist as she felt herself imprisoned relentlessly in a blanket and carried.

The fact that he didn't say a word simply confirmed her belief that it was all part of the dream. She felt too bemused, too tired to ask herself why she could feel his heart pounding, or why he looked so angry.

She protested just a little as he put her down, and was vaguely aware that she was in her bedroom, that Sam wasn't wearing a jacket and that there were flakes of snow glistening in his hair.

She tried to stand, but her legs seemed to have turned to jelly. She swayed and was held instantly, drawn against the taut muscular body.

'Dammit, woman! Your head's bleeding. Just sit still.' His voice brooked no argument as she began to protest. 'Have you any idea of the hell I've been through, wondering why you didn't get back to the surgery? Imagining all sorts of things. If Ruth hadn't told me you were expected back…'

Jaimie stared at his grim face and burst into tears. It was too much. As if she didn't feel bad enough, without having him bellowing at her like an angry bull. With a muttered oath he slipped his arm round her and she felt herself held tightly. 'I'm sorry,' he said softly. He brushed the tears gently from her eyes, before easing her down onto the bed again. 'I'm sorry, Jaimie. I didn't mean to shout at you, but my imagination has been running riot.' He glanced round the room which, like the sitting room, had been expertly ransacked. 'What the hell happened here, Jaimie?'

If she hadn't been trapped in the warmth of the blanket she would have reached up to brush the hair from his face, to smooth the gaunt, anxious look from his eyes, but he sat beside her, holding her against him.

She gulped hard. 'I decided to come back to the cottage to get a drink and some aspirins.' Her voice shook. 'When I got here I noticed that the door was open. S-someone was in here.'

She choked back a small sob. 'I must have surprised him. He came hurtling down the stairs and I was in the way. That's why I fell. I don't remember anything after that.'

Sam swore softly, his fingers gently probing the wound at her temple. 'You're going to have a nasty bruise there, I'm afraid, and you're suffering from shock.'

Which had to be why she was feeling so tearful, she told herself. 'I'll be fine.' She sniffed hard. 'It's just this headache.'

He looked at her and frowned. 'I'm afraid, my darling, that on top of everything else you've caught a nasty dose of flu, and it's probably all my fault.'

It probably was, she thought crossly, then anger faded as he kissed her very gently, before handing her a glass of water and a couple of tablets and watching as she swallowed them.

'Don't worry, I'm going to see you tucked up safely in bed.'

'That will be nice,' she murmured contentedly, only protesting when within minutes he plumped the pillows vigorously before settling her gently against them.

'I hope they catch him,' she said sleepily.

The bed dipped suddenly as it took Sam's weight. His fingers gently brushed a wisp of hair from her face. 'Jaimie, are you saying you saw him?'

She stifled a jaw-cracking yawn, closed her eyes and nodded, tugging the duvet up to her chin. 'I'm so tired.'

'Jaimie, this is important.'

'Tired.'

'I need to know, Jaimie,' Sam persisted. 'Do you know the man? Had you seen him before?'

She sighed and would have looked at him, but her eyes felt strangely heavy. 'At the surgery. I told him we were closed.'

'But do you know his name?'

She thought about it, which wasn't easy as her head seemed to be clogged with a swirling fog. 'Jessle. No, Jessop. He said his name…his mother's name was Jessop.' She forced her eyes open. 'But we didn't have a Mrs Jessop, Sam.'

He smiled and bent forward to brush his lips softly

against her mouth. 'It's all right, my darling. I'll take care of it. You'll soon be asleep now. I just have to go and make a couple of phone calls.'

Within minutes, it seemed, someone was helping her to undress and slide between the blissfully cool sheets. The relief was exquisite. Suddenly she realised that her entire body was aching and she felt ridiculously close to tears again.

'I'm sorry,' she gulped. 'I just need to sleep for a while, then I'm sure I'll be fine in the morning.'

'Somehow I doubt that,' Sam said calmly, and she opened her eyes to find him staring down at her with a kind of brooding expression that made her feel hot and very confused.

She wondered vaguely why he was in her bedroom, then there was a tap on the door and Mrs Barnes came in with a mug of cocoa, clucking sympathetically as she put it on the bedside table and eyed Jaimie.

'You poor thing. It must have been a terrible experience. Well, you're not to worry. I'll have the mess cleared up in no time.' Her glance rose to Sam. 'You were right to call me, Doctor. You managed all right, then?'

'Perfectly, thank you, Mrs Barnes.'

Jaimie wondered briefly what he had managed, then gave up the attempt to work it out as his arm slid behind her and he held her while she finished the drink.

Lying back, she studied him sleepily. It was a pity about Helen Forbes, she thought. She wasn't his type at all.

The phone rang. 'I'll get that for you, Doctor.'

Seconds later, Mrs Barnes's voice drifted up to her. 'If that's a call, tell them I'll—'

'Don't worry about it,' Sam's voice murmured softly in her ear, then she felt his lips brush against her cheek. She felt cheated. Her mouth had been ready for a kiss.

She shivered uncontrollably and heard his sharp intake of breath as he bent towards her. Then Mrs Barnes was in the room again, peering round the door to whisper, 'Oh, Doctor, I'm sorry, but there was a call for Dr Grant. It was Mr Duncan. I explained that's she's not well. I wasn't sure whether you would want me to go into details. He said to give her his love, and he'll call again tomorrow.'

Jaimie felt the happiness die within her as Sam's expression hardened. She began to cry quietly and for a moment her hand was enveloped in a stronger one.

'Stay with me.' She sniffed. 'I don't want you to go.'

There was a moment's hesitation before he answered and then his voice sounded strange. 'I think I'd better. You're not thinking clearly right now and I'm afraid if I stay I might do something we'd both regret in the cold light of day.'

He rose to his feet, cool and withdrawn again. 'Remember me to Giles. Sleep tight, little one. I'm only sorry…'

She couldn't imagine what he was sorry about and suddenly felt far too tired to ponder on it.

'Hello, Giles. Yes, I'm fine. Much better, thank you.'

'I was worried about you, darling, especially when I heard what had really happened. It must have been awful.'

'Yes.' Jaimie smiled slightly. 'It was rather. Not something I'd like to go through again. Still, the good news is that they've caught the man responsible. It seems Jessop was his grandmother's name.'

'Poor darling. I was coming round but Mrs Barnes said you were sleeping and Sam insisted that you needed a real rest.'

'Sam did?'

'Yes. I spoke to him yesterday. He seemed rather edgy, but I suppose he's got his hands full with this epidemic.'

'Yes, I suppose that's it.' Her voice stuck in her throat. 'Still, I'm better now so I'll be taking my share again, which should help.'

'I can't help feeling that you're rushing things. Why not take another day off?'

'It's a nice idea, but I've already had three.' She managed to laugh but it had seemed like three years, lying there, trying to get things into perspective.

'Giles, I was wondering, did you phone the cottage or did I imagine it? I know it sounds silly but things are still a bit hazy.'

'No, you didn't imagine it. I phoned to say thank you for a lovely evening at Jon Reynolds's, and Mrs Barnes answered. She told me you were poorly so I said I'd call back. I wish she'd told me what had really happened.' There was a hint of peevishness in his voice.

'I see.' Jaimie swallowed hard. So that part at least had been real, which meant that the rest… Her fingers toyed with the pen she was holding. 'I expect she didn't want to worry you. Giles—'

'Jaimie, I need to talk to you. I need to see you.' There was a sense of urgency in his voice which suddenly filled her with a sense of foreboding.

'Giles, can it wait until this evening or is it important? Only I am rather busy.' She didn't know why she lied, except that for some reason she preferred not to identify she didn't want him to say what she was sure he was going to say.

There was a slight pause at the other end of the line.

'Actually, it is rather important, unless you'd rather it waited?'

'No.' She swallowed hard. 'It's all right. Go ahead.'

'It's just that, well, we were rather interrupted the other night. We didn't exactly finish our conversation, did we?'

Poor Giles. She could sense his uncertainty and her hands tightened. 'No, I suppose we didn't.'

'I seem to make a habit of it, getting my timing all wrong, don't I?' There was a hollow ring to his laughter. 'The truth is, Jaimie, I do love you. You know that, don't you?'

'Yes, I think I do, Giles, but—'

'I told myself I wouldn't rush things. It's just that—'

'Giles, I—'

'I know, you don't have to tell me. I'm not being fair.' He rushed on without giving her a chance to speak. 'But the truth is, ever since we met I've known you were something special, that I wanted you in my life, Jaimie. As more than just a friend. The other evening, when I asked you to marry me, I was perfectly serious.'

The tightness in her throat was suddenly threatening to choke her. 'Yes, I realise that, Giles, and I'm very flattered that you should think of me in that way.' Why couldn't he make things easier? Surely he must know that she wasn't capable of making a rational decision right now? She caught sight of her face in the mirror. It looked thinner, pale.

'Jaimie, darling, I don't want to push, but the uncertainty is driving me crazy. I want you to say yes. Darling, I know I could make you happy.'

'Oh, Giles.' She didn't doubt for one second that if she married him she would be secure and cared for. But was that enough? 'I'm sure you could. You're a good man, Giles. It isn't that. I'm very fond of you. You'll always be special.'

There was a long pause and then he said huskily, 'You're turning me down, aren't you?'

'Oh, Giles, I wish, I really wish, I could give you the answer you want.' The words came out in a rush. 'I have thought about it. I want you to know that. And I do love you in a way, but not the way you want.'

'I've rushed you, haven't I? Perhaps if I gave you more time?'

'No, it isn't that.' She couldn't bear the hurt in his voice.

'I see. Is…is there someone else?'

She flinched, caught off guard. 'No. There's no one else. As a matter of fact, I shall be leaving Felldale soon. My job here was only temporary anyway. I need to start looking for something more permanent. I've applied for a couple of posts.'

It wasn't true, but the irony of it was that, even as she said it, she knew she would have to leave now anyway because she couldn't bear to go on living and working so close to Sam, knowing that he was in love with someone else.

Giles seemed to be waging his own silent, private

war with himself at the other end of the phone. For a moment she thought he had hung up, then he said quietly, 'I hadn't realised Jon had made such a good recovery.'

'No, he hasn't, not yet.' Jaimie tapped the pen against the desk. 'But when I took the job it was on the understanding that it was just until they could come up with an alternative, preferably someone to join the practice on a permanent basis. In any case...' she bit at her lower lip '...Sam and I haven't exactly hit it off. You must have noticed.'

'I can't say I had.' He gave a slight laugh. 'As a matter of fact, I was beginning to get the idea that he'd taken a fancy to you.'

'Sam! Oh, Giles, you're not serious?' In spite of herself she laughed. 'I think you'll find his interests lie elsewhere.'

'Well, I can only say that I think he's a fool.'

'Oh, Giles.' She heard him draw a deep breath.

'Don't say anything. I might think there's a chance you'll change your mind out of pity if nothing else.'

'I wouldn't do that. You wouldn't want me to do that.'

'I'm not so sure.' His voice rasped, then he said, in an attempt at lightness, 'Anyway, I'm sure you've things to do. I'd better let you get back to your patients.' There was a brief silence. 'So this is goodbye, then, Jaimie. I wish you luck and I hope we can still be friends.'

The receiver clicked before she could say anything in reply. Staring at it, she toyed briefly with the idea of calling him back to say she didn't want things to end like that.

But it was no use. She didn't love Giles. She loved

Sam, with all his stubbornness and arrogant pride. And there was no future in that, no future at all. The only thing left to do was to go away, try to pick up the pieces and start again.

She managed to avoid seeing Sam for the rest of the morning, but in the early afternoon, when she returned to collect some papers, her heart missed a beat as she saw Helen's car parked in front of the surgery.

They had probably been out to lunch. The thought lingered with her like a black cloud as Jaimie slipped as quietly as possible through Reception and to her own room. She was annoyed with herself for having forgotten the papers.

The waiting room was quiet now that the patients had gone. Chairs lined the room. Magazines sat in a neat pile on the table; toys had been returned to their box. It all looked unnaturally tidy, and for the first time she was hit by the sudden realisation that she was going to miss all of this. In the past few weeks it had become part of her life.

Worse than that, she was going to miss Sam. There was going to be a huge void in her life which no amount of work could fill. But somehow she had to try and the sooner she got away the better. There was no point in fooling herself that her feelings for Sam would ever change. The most she could hope for was that, by making a fresh start, she would learn to live without him.

She had reached the decision the previous night, after hours of lying awake, staring at the ceiling. All that remained was to find the right moment to broach the subject.

Jon would understand that she needed to look for

something more permanent. Sam was scarcely a consideration. He would be glad to see her go.

Jaimie dropped the papers she had come to collect into her bag. Glancing round the room, she picked up a medical journal. Flicking through it earlier, she had seen an advertisement for doctors needed to work overseas. It wasn't something she had considered until now.

She was crossing Reception when she heard the muffled sound of voices, and realised that Sam's door was open slightly. She heard Helen's voice. It was edged with annoyance.

'Sam, whether you like it or not, there's a big world out there. You can't shut yourself away and pretend it doesn't exist. I know you loved Sara, but she's dead, Sam, and you have to get on with your life. I'm not asking you to forget her, but you can't throw away any chance of happiness just because you're afraid it will happen all over again.'

Involuntarily, Jaimie froze to the spot. Her feet wouldn't move, not even when she heard Sam's voice, suddenly very close, as if he was standing just the other side of the door.

'I know you're right.' There was a taut edge to the words. 'I've tried to forget her.'

'You don't have to forget her, Sam. Just move on.'

'I suppose I've been kidding myself that I owed it to her memory in some way. I realise now that I was just being a coward.'

'No, that isn't true. A little mixed-up, maybe.'

'I've always felt that I'd be betraying Sara in some way by marrying.'

'Oh, Sam, darling, don't you realise that's what Sara would have wanted you to do? She would have hated to see you waste your life. She loved you. She would have wanted you to be happy, you must know that.'

'It's taken a while, but, yes, I do. I'm only sorry I've wasted so much time.'

Jaimie could feel herself trembling. With an effort she forced herself to move. Her hand was shaking as she reached the door.

It was decided, then? He was going to marry Helen. It only served to deepen her resolve. The sooner she got away the better, before she made a complete fool of herself.

To her horror she missed her footing, stumbling against a chair. For an instant she froze, hoping it hadn't been heard, then suddenly Sam was standing framed in the doorway of his room, his face taut as he called after her.

'Jaimie, wait.'

She resolutely ignored him. She didn't want to hear what he had to say, didn't care that he was angry because she had been eavesdropping.

Tears coursed down her cheeks. She flung herself into the car, grated the gears and swore under her breath, all too conscious of the figure reflected in her driving mirror as she drove away.

Later that evening, after she had drawn the curtains in the cottage, she sat down in front of the fire and tried to write her letter of resignation. It wasn't easy, but an hour later the brief, stiffly formal letter was finished. It was the best she could do. No excuses, no tears, or at least none that would be seen. A clean ending.

She went to bed, leaving the letter on the table beside her bag, and, in spite of her fears, fell asleep the instant her head touched the pillow.

CHAPTER THIRTEEN

EXHAUSTION and nervous tension had finally set in so that, for the first time in days, Jaimie slept soundly. So soundly, in fact, that it took several minutes for the loud shrilling of the phone to penetrate her sleep-fogged brain.

Groaning into her pillow, she opened one eye to stare disbelievingly at the clock. *Two-thirty a.m.* She felt shaky and drugged as she reached out a hand and fumbled for the bedside lamp, then the receiver, and said huskily, 'Dr Grant.'

'Oh, Doctor, this is Felldale General Hospital here.' A woman's voice spoke coolly in her ear. 'Sister Thorn speaking. I'm sorry to have to disturb you but I thought you would want to be informed. I'm afraid I have bad news.'

Jaimie was wide awake now, standing on legs that trembled as she tried to gather her wits. Not Sam, please, don't let it be Sam.

'I'm afraid Dr Reynolds has been brought in as an emergency admission, Doctor.'

Jaimie's mouth suddenly felt very dry. She had to moisten her lips with her tongue before she could speak. 'Not another heart attack?'

'It's a little too early to say. He's complaining of chest pains, but the consultant is with him now. Obviously, in view of his past history, we're rather concerned. We thought you would want to know.'

'Yes, I'm very grateful. I— Is anyone with him now?'

'Not at this moment. Mrs Barnes, his housekeeper, called the ambulance and came with him.'

'How is she?'

'Very upset, naturally. I gather she found the doctor. It was lucky she heard him and managed to get help so quickly. She was in a state of shock, understandably, so I suggested she go home rather than sit here. It's not as if she can do anything, but she would only agree to leave if I promised to call you and Dr Reynolds's partner. I've been trying to reach Dr Paige for some time now to let him know, but he must be out on a call.'

'Yes, I'm sure that's it.' Jaimie raked a hand through her hair. 'Look, I'll be there as soon as I can. Give Dr Reynolds my love. Tell him I'm on my way.'

Minutes later she was heading for the bathroom, struggling into her clothes as she gulped at a strong, black coffee to wake herself up.

She found a pair of jeans and a shirt, then a sweater which she pulled on over the top. Her thoughts were in turmoil. Uncle Jon had seemed so much better. It was inconceivable that he might die and yet she knew enough not to fool herself that it might not happen.

The drive to the hospital seemed interminable. She kept praying that someone had been able to contact Sam. She didn't know if she could cope with this alone. It was going to hit him hard too.

Minutes later she pulled into the car park where the lights cast a strange glow over everything. A cold wind whipped through the trees and she climbed, shivering, out of the car. There was no sign of Sam's car and her spirits sank.

So they still hadn't been able to reach him. Perhaps he was with Helen, she thought bleakly, then shut the idea out of her mind. It was none of her business what he did with his free time.

But there was something unnerving about walking along the corridors, listening to the sound of her own shoes on the gleaming floor as she hurried towards the swing doors.

She caught sight of a navy-blue-clad figure coming towards her. 'Sister.'

'Dr Grant? I'm so sorry we had to call you.'

'I'm glad you did.' There was still no sign of Sam and suddenly she wanted him there, very much. Her throat felt tight and painful. 'How is he? I'd like to know before I go in to see him.' She tried to smile but her lips felt stiff with tension. 'I promise I won't let him see that I'm upset.'

Sister Thorn considered her gravely, slowing her steps a little. 'I'm sure you won't. I'm afraid it isn't good news. He's had another heart attack.'

'Oh, no.' Jaimie swallowed hard on the tightness in her throat. 'Is he conscious?'

'Yes, he is, but we'd rather he didn't try to talk. What he needs more than anything right now is to rest. You're very welcome to go in and see him but Doctor has given him something to help him relax and would prefer it if he got some sleep.'

Jaimie's hands shook as she braced herself to enter the room. 'I promise I won't encourage him to talk. I'll just take a look at him.' She paused at the door of the small side ward. 'I don't suppose anyone has been able to contact Dr Paige?'

'Not yet, as far as I know. I'll go and make some enquiries for you.' Sister smiled and nodded towards the door. 'Go in. Sit by the bed for a while. I expect he'll feel happier, just knowing that you're there. Nurse will be popping in and out just to see how he's doing.' She hurried away and Jaimie walked slowly into the room.

She'd imagined she'd been prepared but couldn't completely stifle a feeling of shock as she looked at Jon.

He seemed somehow smaller. Lying there, propped up against the pillows, he seemed older, frighteningly more frail, in striking contrast to the man who had seemed so full of life only a few days ago. His face was grey and he lay with his eyes closed.

Jaimie sat in the chair, watching as he slept. A nurse came into the room several times, checking the various monitors, smiling at Jaimie, and going about her tasks with gentle efficiency.

She had lost track of time, even dozed a little, when Sister returned to find her sitting huddled in the chair, biting back tears of frustration that it should have happened to someone she loved so much.

Sister touched her gently on the shoulder and whispered, 'Why don't you go and get yourself a cup of tea? I'm sure you could do with a break and he's sleeping quite peacefully at the moment.'

Jaimie stared at her then rose wearily to her feet. She brushed a hand through her hair. 'I could do with a cup of tea, but you will call me...?'

'Of course, although he's likely to sleep for several hours. It will be better for him if he does.'

Jaimie smiled waveringly. 'I'll be in the coffee-lounge if you need to find me. I know I can't do anything, but I'd like to stay for a while, just to know that he's all right.'

'I understand perfectly and, I promise, if there's any change at all I'll come and find you.'

'You're very kind.' Jaimie moved away, scarcely knowing where she was going, wishing desperately there was someone she could talk to.

The vending machine gave out a plastic beaker of watery brown liquid which could have been anything, but at least it was hot and sweet. Her hands were shaking as she sank into one of the large chairs and stared at the clock. Four o'clock. If he got through tonight... Please, let him get through the night.

Jaimie closed her eyes. Somewhere close by doors swished open and closed. She didn't look up as footsteps approached, then, thinking it might be Sister Thorn, she rose unsteadily to her feet.

'Sam.' Without realising it she was in his arms and being held tightly and he was stroking her hair. 'Oh, Sam, I'm so glad you're here.'

'It's all right. I came as quickly as I could.' Holding her hands, he led her back to the chair. 'What happened?'

For the first time as he looked at her she saw the lines of desperate tiredness in his face. 'I just got back from seeing a patient when the hospital called.'

'It's Jon.' Her voice trembled. 'He's had another heart attack.'

'Oh, God... I must go and see him. Have you...?' He looked at her. 'He *is* all right?'

She nodded. 'They've sedated him. He's sleeping. But he looks so desperately ill, Sam. I couldn't bear it if he—'

'Don't.' His voice rasped and with a quick movement he bent and kissed her. 'Don't, Jaimie. You've got to believe that he's going to make it. We both have.'

'I want to.' She brushed a hand over her eyes. 'I just wanted so much for you to be here.'

He brushed the hair gently back from her face. 'You don't imagine they could have kept me away?'

She was on her feet, swaying with tiredness. 'I have to go back and see him. You will come with me, won't you? Please, Sam, I can bear it if you're with me.'

He studied her grimly. 'I've no intention of going anywhere. You needn't worry that I shall ever leave you again.'

It was comforting to have his arm around her. Somewhere it registered in her brain that he hadn't been out with Helen after all.

They had just walked through the swing doors when Sister Thorn came hurrying towards them. Jaimie felt her heart miss a beat and instinctively Sam's arm tightened round her.

'I'm with you, Jaimie,' he murmured gruffly, but she could see the sudden tightening of his own mouth as he hurried her along the corridor, the sound of their footsteps echoing in the night stillness.

'Oh, Dr Paige, they managed to contact you, then.' Sister Thorn smiled in recognition. 'I was just coming to find Dr Grant.'

Jaimie felt her knees buckle and would have fallen if Sam hadn't held her. 'He's not…?' She couldn't bring herself to say the word and was aware of Sam's white face above her own.

Incredibly, Sister smiled. 'No, Doctor, he's fine.'

Jaimie closed her eyes and felt some of the tension slip out of Sam's hold upon her. 'Oh, thank God.'

'In fact, that's why I came to find you. Yes, there has been a change—very slight, of course, but you'll be pleased to hear that he's breathing much more easily and is sleeping quite peacefully.'

She smiled. 'I was going to suggest that you might want to think about going home for a few hours and trying to get some rest. There's really nothing you can do here and I promise I'll call you if there's any change at all.' She looked at them both. 'I'm sure you don't need me to tell you that we often get an instinct about these things, and mine tells me that Dr Reynolds is going to be all right.'

Sam looked at Jaimie. She knew her face was pale and her eyes raw from the lack of sleep but she was past caring.

'Thank you, Sister,' Sam said quietly. 'I think we'll take your advice, for a few hours at least.' He drew Jaimie's coat gently around her shoulders. His hands turned the collar up. 'Come on. I'm taking you home.'

She felt too drained to ask where 'home' was. She sat in the car, letting the feeling of tiredness wash over her. She was glad when he made no attempt to start the engine and they just sat in the semi-darkness.

'He is going to be all right, isn't he, Sam?'

'I think he is.' He smiled. 'You know Jon. He won't give up without a fight.'

She turned to look at him. 'I was so afraid. I didn't know how I'd face it without you.' She buried her face in her hands but suddenly she was in his arms again and he was kissing her fiercely, possessively, as if to shut out all the doubts. 'Darling, darling Jaimie.' His voice was gruff as he released her for a moment. 'If you only knew how I felt when I got that call and realised you were here, facing this alone. I drove like a maniac and when I saw you just sitting there I thought… Oh, my God, I thought…' His hands gripped her shoulders. 'I love you, you know that, don't you?'

Her answer was muffled by yet another kiss. She could scarcely believe what was happening. Perhaps even now it was all part of the nightmare and when she opened her eyes he would have vanished. Her hands held him away.

'But what about Helen?' The words were torn from her in desperation. 'You're going to marry Helen. How can you love me?'

He was staring at her incredulously. 'Helen? You're not serious. For heaven's sake, where does she come into this?'

'But…but I thought… I heard you talking…about marriage.'

She heard his swift exclamation of impatience. 'My darling girl, if you had listened to the entire conversation, instead of running away, you might have realised that it wasn't Helen I intended to marry, but you.'

'Me?' Her eyes widened.

'Well, who else?'

'But I thought…'

'Yes, I realise now what you must have thought and I'm furious with myself for not going after you and making you listen. But the truth is that after Sara died I really thought I would never want to think about marriage again. It was Helen who made me realise what a fool I was, that I was running the risk of losing you because of it.'

Jaimie stared at him. 'She said that?'

He laughed softly. 'Helen happens to be Sara's sister, my love. Since Sara died of meningitis she has kept me sane.'

'Oh, Sam.' Jaimie gulped hard. 'I'm so sorry. It must have been awful for you.'

His mouth twisted. 'I think you could say I went a little haywire for a time. It was the speed of it all that I found so hard to take in. Sara was a lecturer at the university. One of the students was rushed to hospital with suspected meningitis. Over the next few days there were another two cases and then…it was Sara.'

He shook his head. 'One minute we were making wedding plans and the next… I'm a doctor. I'm supposed to know about these things, but I couldn't take in what was happening.'

'It's always different when it's personal, Sam.' Her hand rested gently over his and he took her fingers into his strong, warm grasp. 'You must have missed her dreadfully.'

'It left a gap in my life,' he said softly. 'I can't pretend it didn't. But they're right. Time does lessen the pain and I had to get on with my life. I know it's what Sara would have wanted.'

He bent his head to brush his lips against hers and looked at her, his eyes glittering. 'I can't promise you that I'll forget Sara. She was something very special in my life. But I *have* moved on, Jaimie, my darling.'

She shook her head, feeling the tears well up in her eyes. 'Sam, you don't have to do this…'

'I want to,' he said huskily. 'I want you to know that what I feel for you is very special, too. It's different. It's good, very good, Jaimie.'

His thumb gently stroked her cheek. 'Helen made me see that life doesn't stop because someone you love goes away, and I realise now that she was right.'

Jaimie couldn't speak. It was all too much to take in.

Sam put a finger under her chin, forcing her to look at him. 'What about you and Giles?'

She laughed. 'Oh, yes, Giles.'

'He asked you to marry him.'

'And I said no.' Her hands touched his face, teased the hair at the nape of his neck, and she heard him moan softly before he gathered her up fiercely into his arms. 'I had to say no. I want to spend the rest of my life with someone I love. And I love you, my darling, if you want me.'

His answer was a kiss which seemed to go on for ever, and which left her in no doubt at all what the answer would be.

MILLS & BOON®

Makes any time special

**Enjoy a romantic novel from
Mills & Boon®**

Presents...™ *Enchanted*™ TEMPTATION.

Historical Romance™ ◄ MEDICAL
ROMANCE™

MILLS & BOON®

MEDICAL ROMANCE™

MOTHER TO BE by Lucy Clark

Dr Mallory Newman had always loved surgeon Nicholas Sterling but when he married her best friend, she was devastated. Now he's back, widowed and with a two year old daughter. Can his determination to win Mallory's heart survive what she has to tell him first?

DOCTORS AT ODDS by Drusilla Douglas

The last person Dr Sarah Sinclair had wanted to see on her return home was orthopaedic registrar Rory Drummond. After all, her unrequited love for him had caused her to leave in the first place. Had time changed anything or were they destined to be just friends?

A SECOND CHANCE AT LOVE by Laura MacDonald

Single mother Dr Olivia Chandler has no choice but to offer locum Dr Duncan Bradley her spare room. His resemblance to her daughter's father is unsettling but as she gets to know him, she finds herself loving him for himself. But is the feeling mutual?

Available from 7th July 2000

0006/03a

MILLS & BOON®

MEDICAL ROMANCE™

HEART AT RISK by Helen Shelton

Luke Geddes' appointment as Consultant Cardiologist brings him directly in contact with his ex-wife, Dr Annabel Stuart. Shocked at her change in appearance, he is dismayed to discover that what he thought was a mutual parting, was anything but for her...

GREATER THAN RICHES by Jennifer Taylor
Bachelor Doctors

Dr Alexandra Campbell is sure that Dr Stephen Spencer won't be able to cope with helping out the inner city practice. Continually at cross purposes, it's not until Stephen puts his life in danger for Alex that she finally discovers her feelings may be deeper than she thought.

MARRY ME by Meredith Webber
Book Three of a Trilogy

Dr Sarah Gilmour's new posting to Windrush Sidings brought back many memories. Seeing Tony Kemp, the love of her life, after eleven years forced her to realise how much he meant to her. Yet, for now, she needed his help as a senior police officer with an unexpected death...

Available from 7th July 2000

Available at most branches of WH Smith, Tesco, Martins, Borders, Easons, Volume One/James Thin and most good paperback bookshops

FREE

4 BOOKS
AND A SURPRISE GIFT!

We would like to take this opportunity to thank you for reading this Mills & Boon® book by offering you the chance to take FOUR more specially selected titles from the Medical Romance™ series absolutely FREE! We're also making this offer to introduce you to the benefits of the Reader Service™—

★ FREE home delivery   ★ FREE gifts and competitions
★ FREE monthly Newsletter   ★ Exclusive Reader Service discounts
★ Books available before they're in the shops

Accepting these FREE books and gift places you under no obligation to buy; you may cancel at any time, even after receiving your free shipment. Simply complete your details below and return the entire page to the address below. *You don't even need a stamp!*

YES! Please send me 4 free Medical Romance books and a surprise gift. I understand that unless you hear from me, I will receive 6 superb new titles every month for just £2.40 each, postage and packing free. I am under no obligation to purchase any books and may cancel my subscription at any time. The free books and gift will be mine to keep in any case.

MOEC

Ms/Mrs/Miss/Mr ....Initials ....
BLOCK CAPITALS PLEASE

Surname ....

Address ....

....

....Postcode ....

Send this whole page to:
UK: FREEPOST CN81, Croydon, CR9 3WZ
EIRE: PO Box 4546, Kilcock, County Kildare (stamp required)

Offer valid in UK and Eire only and not available to current Reader Service subscribers to this series. We reserve the right to refuse an application and applicants must be aged 18 years or over. Only one application per household. Terms and prices subject to change without notice. Offer expires 31st December 2000. As a result of this application, you may receive further offers from Harlequin Mills & Boon Limited and other carefully selected companies. If you would prefer not to share in this opportunity please write to The Data Manager at the address above.

Mills & Boon® is a registered trademark owned by Harlequin Mills & Boon Limited.
Medical Romance™ is being used as a trademark.

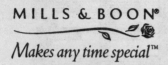